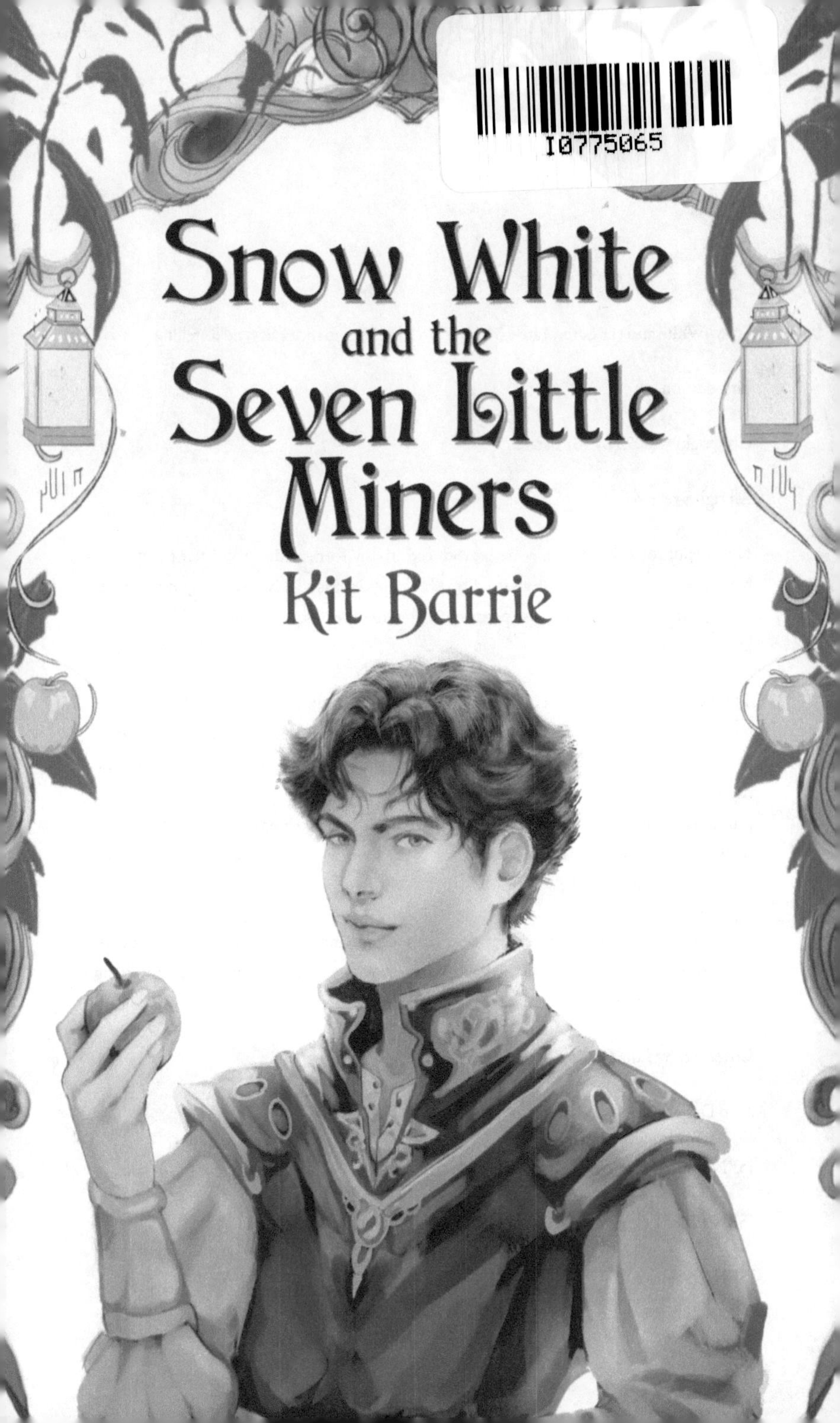

Snow White
and the
Seven Little Miners

Kit Barrie

CONTENTS

Content Warning

This story contains main character fairytale-style deaths (both permanent and non), attempted murder (knife and strangulation,) poisoning, talk of women and children being killed, famine, non-graphic hunting of animals, emotional abuse by a parent, and off-page loss of family and friends.

Author's Note: The term 'little men' was chosen rather than dwarfs or dwarves for two reasons. First, the term 'little people' is the correct and preferred way to refer to individuals of smaller stature, as not all little people have dwarfism. Second, due to the fairytale nature of the story, the use of 'dwarf' might present confusion to readers. The little people in this story are entirely human.

Varinien
Hallin
Hallin Castle
Cinder's Estate
Frog Prince's Lair
N
W
E
S
The GriMM Tales

Falchovari
Evil Queen's Castle
(Rumpelstilzchen's Haunting Grounds)
Shoemaker's Shop
Pied Pipers Music Shop
Sorcerer's Tower
Dark Forest
Miners' House
The Candy House
Mines
Old Oma's House

One

Once upon a time, twenty winters ago, the Queen of Falchovari gave birth to a child, the first and only she ever bore. His hair was as black as a starless night, his skin pale and soft as fresh cream, and his eyes as blue as a summer sky. All of the servants agreed that he was the most beautiful baby they had ever seen, and the Queen was very pleased. She named him Makellos, for he was to be perfection, a flawless gem to emphasize her own beauty.

Queen Schön had ruled Falchovari for almost two hundred years. Despite the unnatural length of her reign, The Queen was ageless and stunningly beautiful, always in good health, with no wrinkles or age spots. The bloom of the rose was always upon her cheeks, the luster of gold was in her hair, and the paleness of the moon was upon her skin. All agreed that she was the fairest, most beautiful person in all of Falchovari.

Despite the beauty that graced her physical form, it was also agreed that inside, the Queen was twisted and ugly and evil. She cared not for the needs of her people, their appeals for lower taxes, help in growing their crops, or protecting them from bandits or the creatures of the Dark Forest. There were still a few who knew her when she was a young apprentice to a famous sorcerer, but those few were dwindling, and none bothered or dared to stand up to the Queen's reign.

For a long time, the citizens of Falchovari were content enough to live their lives without much regard for the Queen and her selfish, mysterious ways. But, for a number of winters now, the kingdom had been struggling. Food was becoming scarcer and scarcer. Game was not as abundant in the forest. The vegetables in the fields grew sickly and sallow. The streams that had once overflowed with fish now were barren.

While children starved in the streets, Queen Schön ate lavish meals on shining gold plates and drank wine from goblets encrusted with jewels. While farmers froze in their homes during the oppressive winters, the Queen had the most beautiful clothing created for her. Early in her reign, the Queen had enslaved a shadow geist. This was difficult to do and only reinforced the strength of the Queen's dark magic, instilling fear throughout the land. She sent him out to deal with anyone who displeased her, dispatching them with brutal efficiency. If there was talk of rebellion or calls for change, the Queen sent her royal guards, or the Thieves Guild that answered to her whims, or her Shadow to quash any talk of discontent.

It was shortly before all of this that Queen Schön became with child. She took for herself a lover; a young nobleman, fair of face, said by some to be the most beautiful man in the kingdom. No one knew how or why she had entranced him into her bed, but no one was surprised either when the fair young man perished under mysterious circumstances in the days after the Queen gave birth to a son.

There was much speculation as to her reason for bearing a child, for the Queen was very vain and had never seemed the maternal sort. Some thought that she had seen a pregnant woman looking so joyous and radiant that she wanted that brilliance for herself. Others whispered that the Queen needed a child for purposes of her dark magic. Still others thought that after so long alone, the Queen was feeling untethered and wanted a child to care for.

The Queen herself never confirmed to anyone the reason behind her choice to finally have a child after so many years, and no one dared to ask. But even though she had gone through the effort to have a child, the Queen did not care for him as a mother would. Prince Makellos was a beautiful gemstone in her crown, nothing more than a trained pet or rare treasure to be paraded around and admired. He was indeed beautiful of face, and his manners were polite and respectful. He was clever and did well at his lessons, and it was often remarked at how gracious he was. But no one dared to assume that the boy prince would one day take over the kingdom from his mother. To say so would be considered treason.

Despite the lack of maternal warmth toward him, the little prince grew to have a kind and cheerful heart, especially towards animals. He loved tending to the horses in the stables, telling them stories as he brushed their coats to shiny perfection or braided their manes with beautiful beads and bows before a big celebration. The barn cats that kept the rodents at bay would hiss and swipe sharp little claws at anyone else who dared approach them, except for the kind prince. They would climb onto his lap and purr, bumping his hand to be petted and accepting bites of dried fish from his fingers.

Sometimes in the stables, the boy prince would catch glimpses of Hans, his mother's huntsman, and sometimes another young servant boy by the name of Red. Red was slightly older than him, with curious-looking eyes. Makellos wondered if he and Red could perhaps be friends. He would have relished a friend close to his own age to play with and get into the sort of mischief young boys did. But Makellos had seen many of the servants come and go, and he knew not all of them left of their own free will. The Queen's temper was legendary, as was her cruelty. It seemed that every time a servant was kind to him, they would soon be gone. This hurt Makellos' heart, losing the few servants that he might consider his friends. As such, he often ignored Red, barely speaking to him, and retreating to his room when the young man was about.

He had learned early on that his mother did not want him to spend time with the servants. They were beneath him, she had said. He was a royal prince, and he needed to act like one. Of course, his only guidance for what royalty should look like was his mother, as there was no king, no nobles, no siblings to turn to for guidance. He tried aloofness with the servants, the way his mother did, but his heart was too tender, and he often made himself cry from how cruel he felt to those who served him. He wanted to be gentle and cheery and helpful, the sort of good person that people liked. He found instead that being solitary and withdrawn kept most of the servants at arm's length, so that was often what he did, and his quiet reclusiveness only continued as he grew older. There was only one exception to that self-imposed isolation.

One of the palace servants, Auntie Anne, would often meet Makellos in the kitchen late at night, when the Queen was asleep. They had originally crossed paths when Makellos was still a youth, sneaking down to the pantry for some apples, his favorite fruit. That single chance meeting as Auntie Anne had been rolling out the dough for an apple pie had sparked something inside of him, something that excited him. He discovered through Auntie Anne's lessons that he loved to cook and bake. The Queen would have thought those skills to be far below the young prince's station and might have dismissed Auntie Anne if she had found out, so their meetings and her tutelage were kept a secret only between him and kindly older woman.

Often, Makellos' attempts at baking were served for breakfast in the morning, with Queen Schön none the wiser as to their origin. As Makellos grew older and Auntie Anne grew feebler, Makellos would slip into the kitchen on his own at night and make food that he would leave for the servants: all manners of pastries, breads, stews, and other fare, to ensure that it was not wasted. These excursions in the kitchen were one of his few pleasures in life. Many would think that being born to royalty, the young prince would have an unending supply of delights and vices. But the Queen was adamant that Makellos associate as little as possible with the servants, and even less so with the citizens of the kingdom. The kitchens of the palace became one of his only escapes from his otherwise highly regulated and regimented life.

As a child, he often found himself dirty, as children are wont to do, whether it was smudged ink on his sleeves from his lessons or dirt on his pants from riding horses. It was unbecoming of a son of the beautiful, vain Queen to be unsuitable in front of any visiting guests, or even the servants. The final straw for her had been at a grand party for some visiting dignitary when Makellos had arrived inside, covered in hay and dust from the stables. His mother had scolded him for letting himself be seen in such a state and had ordered him to change. The young prince had tried so quickly to obey that he got in his own way, tripped, and took down a table full of delicate desserts (several of which he had helped make.) Cream and fruit and pastry went everywhere, covering him nearly from head to toe in sweet, sticky cream. Everyone had had a good laugh, even Makellos, for who wouldn't find it funny for a gawky young boy to have whipped cream and blueberries in his hair?

His mother, on the other hand, had been mortified. The very next day, she summoned Makellos to her private chambers. It was the first time he had ever been allowed in her rooms, and he marveled at the novelty of it. Once they were alone, she led him over to a large armoire against one wall near the bed. It was made of a dark wood, and on the doors was a large painted peacock, covered in hundreds, perhaps even thousands, of shimmering gemstones, mostly sapphires and emeralds. It was so glittery and shiny, he couldn't resist reaching out a hand to try to touch it. His mother slapped his hand and pointed to the edge of the bed nearby.

Makellos rubbed at his hand and tried not to cry. He turned his back on her to walk to the bed, and he heard something click, followed by the sound of the cabinet doors opening. He sat down on the edge of the bed as he watched his mother step inside the wardrobe. He couldn't see what was inside from where he sat, so he wiggled his way down to the foot of the bed and leaned over as much as he could. He still couldn't see beyond the first step, which seemed to be a stone floor, but he could see the irregular flicker of torches on the wall. It must be a secret room, he thought. One that only his mother knew about. He knew his mother practiced magic, and it made sense to him that she would need a special space in which to do so. He was curious to see the inside of the chamber for himself, but he was a good and obedient child, so he stayed on the bed where he had been commanded.

Queen Schön returned with a book of magic spells, and she used several large, beautiful stones to cast an enchantment on him that Makellos didn't understand. After that day in her chambers, every article of clothing that Makellos ever wore was enchanted to always be clean and pressed, no matter what the young prince did. Dirt, dust, stains, anything considered unsightly vanished almost instantly. It provoked whispers amongst the servants that the prince was treated more like a porcelain doll than a child and also further reinforced the separation between him and the lowly servants. It did, at least, make it easier for him to hide his nocturnal adventures in the kitchen without fear of errant flour or grease spots to give him away.

As he grew older, Makellos began to realize how sheltered his life had been as the only prince of Falchovari. It pained him that he did not know the people of his own kingdom. He rarely was allowed to leave the palace, and much of what he knew of the world outside its walls were what he heard as whispers from the servants. His tutors tried to educate him on the policies and laws of the land, but all of it was subject to the Queen's whim and could change as easily as the wind, depending on her mood. For all the ruling of the people that she did not do, what she did rule, she ruled with an iron fist. Or rather, a diamond one, Makellos thought. His mother was brutal, manipulative, and cruel. Any kindness she showed was carefully calculated to get what she wanted. He grew to recognize it more and more the older he got. He knew the servants whispered about it too. How could such a savage, evil woman like Queen Schön produce such a tender-hearted and sweet child as Prince Makellos? Even he did not have an answer to that.

He did learn as he grew into manhood that food was becoming more and more scarce. He himself never starved; the larders of the palace were always full, the table always laden with platters of meat, fish, fruit, and every delicacy he could imagine. He was never cold, for his clothes were warm, and there was always a cheerful fire burning in the hearth. Though he did not receive love and affection from his mother, his basic needs were always more than fulfilled. "Why do we not share our good fortune with the townspeople?" he asked his mother once.

The Queen had laughed, a sound so condescending it made his teeth ache. "My dear boy, this is the life we lead. All is fair when you wear the crown. If the peasants wish to enjoy more fruits of their labors, they should just work harder."

Makellos didn't think that just working harder would produce crops in lands that were unfertile or populate the rivers with fish again. "It just seems that we could do more to help the-"

"Makellos!" the Queen snapped sharply. "You are young and foolish. You live in a world of wishes, and I do not want to hear another word out of you about these ridiculous notions. You are a prince and my son, and I suggest you behave as such."

"Yes, Mother," he had relented. He had only wanted to help in some way. Wasn't that what royalty was supposed to do? What was the point of having all of the power and money if he didn't share it with those in need? He thought that if perhaps he could get out of the palace, he might be able to do something. He felt stuck here, a porcelain doll kept in a box on a shelf, only brought out to flaunt before being returned to the darkness. Never played with, never allowed to be anything more than a showpiece. He hoped that as he grew to be an adult, he might be able to do more to help the people of Falchovari.

He began to make plans of things he wanted to accomplish. He wanted to meet the people of the country, learn their stories and about how they lived. He wanted to learn some sort of trade that could be helpful. He wanted to find a way to ensure that every person in the kingdom had enough food to stave away hunger and enough clothing to stave away cold. And he wanted to visit other neighboring kingdoms, to see how they were governed and how their people lived.

So, in the autumn of his twentieth year, when he received invitations to attend lavish balls being held in Hallin, their neighboring kingdom to the west, he was delighted. The King and Queen there were seeking a partner for their son, Prince Lorenz. Makellos knew the name, though he had never met the young man. He had once met Prince Adalwin, who had been the crown prince of Hallin a number of winters ago, when Makellos was still a boy. Adalwin had visited the Falchovari court. He had left the palace abruptly to return home, but he never made it back. He vanished along the way and was presumed dead. Makellos wondered what had happened to him, for the Dark Forest that swept through a large swathe of their kingdom was treacherous and full of evil things.

Still, he was hopeful that he might attend at least one of the balls and approached his mother about it when the invitation arrived. "Of course you shall not attend, my dear," the Queen said, her ruby lips curling up into a sneer. "If they are so foolish that they do not ask for your hand outright, we will certainly not entertain this cattle market."

Disappointment surged inside of him. A visit to Hallin, to attend a ball or two with the prince would have been an exciting escape from Falchovari, even for a short time, and might have given him the opportunity to see more of the lands and its people as well. But he could not defy the Queen's wishes. "Yes, Mother," he replied, and not another word was said between them about it.

Two

Queen Schön had always been a powerful user of magic. She had trained for many years under the sorcerer Ulrich, and her magic had grown even stronger in the two hundred years she had ruled Falchovari. In the room off her chambers behind the peacock armoire was her private workspace where she mixed her magic potions and practiced her dark magic. No one was allowed inside or even knew how to enter it.

There was speculation amongst the people of Falchovari as to the secret of her longevity and exquisite features, but there were only a few who knew the truth. Every morning, she drank a vial of magical potion she brewed herself. It was unknown to anyone exactly what was in the potion, for the Queen kept it a closely guarded secret. Magic was more effective when channeled through an object. Even as a girl, Queen Schön had been impassioned by jewels. Diamonds, rubies, emeralds, sapphires, only the best were for her. And so, she infused her magic into these precious stones.

The Queen took these gems and ground them down into a shimmering, silver powder. This powder was kept in a large, glass bottle in her atelier, replenished with gemstones from the southern mountains whenever it ran low. Each morning, she would measure a dose from the bottle into a dram of fresh water. The silver powder would mix in the glass goblet like galaxies of stars, swirling with the infused gems. Drinking this magic potion each morning endowed the Queen with an otherworldly beauty, making her shimmer like a brilliantly cut diamond herself. She had told Makellos, once he was old enough to be entrusted with the secret that kept her alive and thriving, that when he reached the peak of his beauty, she would allow him to sometimes consume the potion as well, to maintain his fairness, for she could not have him grow old and haggard. When that might be, of course, was entirely up to her own inconstant whims.

Also in the Queen's private workroom was a large, gilded mirror. There were mirrors all over the palace, both because Queen Schön was very conceited, and also because she could use them to summon her Shadow to her whenever she wanted. But this particular mirror was only known to her. She had embedded dark magic into it so that the mirror could only speak the truth. But there was only one question that she really cared to ask. "Magic mirror on the wall, who is the fairest of them all?" the vain Queen would ask. And every day for many years, the mirror would reply, "You, my Queen, are the fairest in the land," and the Queen was satisfied.

It was reaching into the cold months of Makellos' twentieth winter when the Queen asked the mirror, as she did every day, "Magic mirror on the wall, who is the fairest of them all?"

"Famed is thy beauty, Majesty," the mirror said. "But another rises like the dawning sun to outshine thy radiance."

The Queen's eyes widened, for the mirror had never spoken such words to her before. Coldness stirred in her cruel heart. She would find this person who was fairer than she and eliminate them. "Reveal their name," she commanded.

"He is known to thee by three names, Majesty," the mirror intoned. "Prince. Son."

The Queen's stomach turned as she realized to whom the mirror was referring. "Makellos," she said at the same time as the mirror.

Blood of her blood. He had done something to make himself fairer than his own mother, even without the daily magical infusion. But she could regain that fairness. Perhaps her tolerance had grown weak after so many years. Though she had already consumed her potion just before consulting the mirror, she set about to mixing another stronger version of the silver tonic with the crushed stones on her workbench next to the mirror.

When her new, stronger mixture was complete, she swallowed down the brew, feeling its magic flow through her, revitalizing her hair, her eyes, her lips, her skin, her figure. She felt refreshed once more, and even more beautiful than she ever had, so she asked the mirror again. "Magic mirror on the wall, who is the fairest of them all?"

"Famed is thy beauty, Majesty," the mirror said, exactly as before. "But another rises like the dawning sun to outshine thy radiance."

The Queen screamed, throwing glass bottles and bejeweled goblets across the room that exploded against the walls. Uncut stones broke in half, revealing glimmering geodes within. She ripped pages from books and flung the books themselves to the floor, all in a savage rage. It could not be, that her own son, the only child she had ever produced, had finally come to fully flower. And not only to bloom, but to surpass her in every way that mattered.

And what a disappointment he had turned out to be. He was soft-headed, with a too-tender heart. He cried when animals were hurt. He wanted to befriend the servants. He was not impressed by her power, her cruelty, her ability to control others, or even her magic. Their only similarity that spoke of their lineage was their beauty of face. Where she was ice, he was sunshine. Where she was calculating, he was clever. Where she ruled through fear, he showered others with kindness. Where she demanded perfection, he was clumsy and sloppy, more in a manner befitting a scullery maid than a prince of Falchovari or her own son.

But how was she to be rid of him? He was so cloistered here in the palace that staging an accident seemed highly unlikely, and there would be far too many witnesses who might try to help. She thought about the Thieves' Guild in the city, but her faith in them recently was tenuous at best. No, she needed someone close that she could trust to deal with this matter, and deal with it away from the palace, where there would be no one around to interrupt.

And then it came to her. A chance to kill two birds with one proverbial stone, as it were. If she sent Hans, her faithful huntsman for many years, out and away to eliminate Makellos, it would also give her the opportunity to send her younger huntsman-in-training, Red, on another special task. He was always eager to prove himself anyway.

She summoned Hans to her massive throne room, dismissing the guards so no one else would overhear their conversation. She would not have anyone else learn of the plan, lest they warn Makellos, for the boy was clever, and servants did talk.

"It is time for Makellos to become a man. Take him into the forest, far from here," Queen Schön said with a haughty wave of her hand. "Go on a hunt, teach him how to use a bow. You have served me well for many years, Hans. I entrust this mission to you."

"Yes, your majesty," Hans replied with a low bow.

"And there, my faithful huntsman, you will kill him." The words left the Queen's ruby lips as cold as ice.

Hans looked up in surprise, certain he must have misheard. "Your majesty?"

The Queen's mouth curved into a cruel smile. "I do not care how or where it is done. But he shall not return to this palace alive. Do you understand me?"

Hans' voice caught in his throat. Makellos was barely more than a boy and of a tender heart and gentle disposition. He had known the prince literally from the day he was born until now. And while the Queen had never been a doting mother, she had at least held a passing impassiveness for her child. An ornament to trot out to guests like a trained monkey or rare treasure. There could only be one reason that came to mind why she would suddenly decide to eliminate such a bauble. The prince was growing to outshine his mother.

Queen Schön quirked one thin brow at him, her smile dropping into a frosty stare. "Are you going to fail me, Hans?"

"No, your majesty," he finally forced out, bowing his head. There had to be a way to complete this task without spilling the prince's blood; he simply had to find it.

"But to ensure you do not fail in this mission, I send you with this." The Queen patted a bejeweled box resting on the throne beside her. It was made of lovely dark wood, inlaid with marble and opal. The clasp of the box was made with a large, red ruby in the shape of a heart. "You will return to me with his liver and lungs, that I may know you have completed your task."

Hans's heart fell, for he would have to provide proof that he had done the sinister deed.

"You have one week," the Queen replied. "If you do not complete your task and return to me within that time, well..." Her threat was left hanging in the air between them, unspoken, but he didn't need to know further.

"Yes, your majesty," he said, bowing his head again. "We shall leave tomorrow morning."

That evening, the Queen summoned Makellos to her chambers. This surprised the prince, for he had not been in his mother's chambers for many years, not since the day she had enchanted him for his clothing to always stay unspoiled. He made his way to her bedchamber, not far down the wing from his own. He rapped lightly upon the door with his knuckles. "Come in, my child," he heard in his mother's musical tone.

The guard at the door opened it for him, and Makellos stepped inside. The room was much the same as he remembered from his childhood. An elegant four-poster bed similar to his own. Glittering jewels upon nearly every surface. His mother loved jewelry and precious stones; she always had on multiple rings and large brooches or necklaces, and earrings that set off her golden blond hair like sunlight. Against the wall near her bed was the tall, elegant armoire of dark wood, its surface covered with meticulously carved gemstones in the shape of a peacock with spread plumage.

"Makellos, how many times must I tell you, it's rude to lurk in doorways." Her back was to him as she sat at her vanity, brushing her blond tresses carefully so it shown like spun gold.

"I'm sorry, Mother," he said and stepped inside, giving her a bow. "You wished to see me?"

"Yes, my dear. Tomorrow I am sending you on an excursion to the forest. Hans shall accompany you and teach you hunting skills." Queen Schön's lips curved into a simpering smile. "Whatever game you find, bring it here. It shall fatten our larders for the winter. Perhaps a stag? Or perhaps you can snare a stoat or two? The shoemaker could make you a new pair of ermine slippers for the winter."

Makellos felt his stomach clench. He knew that many of the people of the kingdom hunted for meat, and even some royalty in other kingdoms did so for sport. But the idea of hunting appalled him. He did not want to kill a living creature, especially if it served no practical application. "I have no desire to hunt, Mother," he said, his voice soft and sweet. "Our own hunters provide us with plenty of game."

The Queen laughed, a high, haughty sound. "Makellos, you are too much of a simple lad. You've been wanting to leave the palace and explore, have you not?"

He *had* been wanting to leave the palace, especially after the disappointment of not attending the balls in Hallin. And Hans had always been kind to him. Certainly *he* would understand his trepidation to kill a living creature and would have pity on him. And if they did catch anything at all, perhaps he could convince his mother that the meat would be better served being distributed to the townsfolk in their own preparations for winter instead. He knew the palace's storerooms were always full. "Yes, Mother," he said with another small bow. "I shall prepare to go with Hans in the morning."

"There's a good boy," Queen Schön said with a small, tight smile.

Makellos found himself distracted again by the glimmering peacock only a short distance away on the armoire doors. He remembered the day not so many years ago when he had seen her walk into this armoire and back out again with a book of spells. He had always been curious to see the actual chamber behind it, but he had never dared to try to find out. The glittering stones almost seemed to entrance him with their gleam. He took several steps toward it, reaching up a hand to stroke over the delicate lines that made up its curving neck.

"Makellos!" the Queen snapped, and he quickly dropped his hand.

He knew the rumors that floated amongst the servants. He knew that his mother was a powerful magic user, one of the strongest that had ever lived. It was why she had been handed down the crown two centuries ago by an old sorcerer named Ulrich, her mentor who had taught her everything she knew about magic. It was why her beauty had not faded in all of these years, and why she always seemed to prosper even when the rest of the kingdom suffered from starvation. He didn't think he was imbued with any magic of his own, but she also had never taught him any. Perhaps it was out of fear that he might grow more powerful than she? He had no idea. He wondered if one day he might get inside that chamber and see for himself if he had magic within him.

She tipped her face toward him for the single customary goodnight kiss she granted him. "Now, run along and get some sleep. Goodbye, my darling."

What an odd thing to say, Makellos thought as he kissed her soft cheek. But he just smiled sweetly in return. "Good night, Mother."

Three

T hey left early the next morning, before the Queen had even risen from her bed. Makellos had barely slept all night. Despite not wanting to participate in the hunt, he was excited to leave the palace and see the kingdom. And it would just be him and Hans, which meant he might actually have the opportunity to talk to some of the people. He was curious to know what life was like outside of a gilded cage. Perhaps he could learn more about how the townsfolk and farmers lived and if there was anything he could do to make their lives a little easier.

Hans was strangely quiet as they rode their horses south, through the towns that surrounded the castle, out into the farmlands, and then into the forest. They traveled for several days, stopping at various inns along the path. Makellos wanted to talk to the people in the inns and taverns, but Hans told him no and kept him moving or in his room at night. They could talk more with the people on the way back, he said, which didn't make as much sense to Makellos, because then they might be traveling with meat that would spoil if they lingered too long, unless they were going to give it to people on the way. But he also didn't want to risk upsetting Hans and make them return home early, so he contented himself with watching from afar and observing the beautiful world outside of the palace walls.

He took it all in with a sort of child-like wonder. The air was crisp and fresh, with scents that changed depending on where they were. Smells of horses and hay and baked bread and evergreen trees played cloyingly with his nose, his eyes roaming as far as they could see. They passed farmlands where he could see people working in fields, harvesting what was left of the meager bounty before the winter struck. He himself had never known true hunger, and the thought that they were desperate for anything left to come out of the ground hurt his tender heart.

Once they entered the southern forest, it grew darker and cooler. They passed along a well-traveled forest path, seeing small shacks and cottages built nearby. They passed by several people chopping wood with axes; another thankless task, Makellos realized. He watched two young men, one with dark hair and the other taller with red hair, a little way apart, chopping and binding wood. He had also never been truly cold, always with warm clothes on his back and a fire lit in his rooms. And he had never had to do the work to keep himself warm either. He tried to be polite and thank the servants when his mother was not around to hear, but he realized he had not given as much thought to the people who farmed and gathered the food and wood and wool and all of the things needed to make his life comfortable.

"Hans, do you think my mother would allow me to travel more within the kingdom? To meet with our people?" he asked pleasantly as their horses trotted along. "I'd like to learn more about how they live. Where our supplies come from, what is involved in such things."

Hans grunted softly, his eyes fixed on the path ahead. "Perhaps."

"Obviously not alone," Makellos continued. "With you, or some of the other guards. Perhaps we could give out things to people in need. We have so much in the palace storehouses. Even with providing for all of the servants, we have more than enough."

He waited for a response, but none came. Makellos wondered if Hans had something on his mind, for he had never known him to be this sullen and withdrawn.

"This way," Hans said, and he suddenly left the well-worn path to go deeper into the trees. Makellos spurred his horse to follow after him. Above his head in the trees, birds chirped, and he heard the rustle of squirrels. Once in a while an animal would dash nearby. A hare, a fox, even a pair of geese with several little downy goslings, who hissed and flapped their wings at Hans but calmed and gazed at Makellos with their dark eyes as they passed by. He smiled at every animal he saw, for he rarely saw one that was alive, much less in the wild. How could anyone think of hurting such beautiful creatures?

After some time trotting through the trees, which had become thicker, and the woods growing progressively darker, Hans slowed his horse near a little cleared patch with a large boulder to break up the bitter wind that blew through the trees. "Here. We shall tie up the horses and make camp," Hans said.

Makellos obediently swung down from his horse, giving her nose a pat and sneaking her a lump of sugar he had hidden away in his pocket. He tied her reigns to a nearby tree, leather boots rustling softly across the leaf-strewn ground. It was growing quite cold, and many of the trees had lost most of their leaves, leaving spindly, dark branches stretching upward into the darkening slate-gray sky.

The hair on the back of Makellos' neck prickled, sensing danger nearby. Perhaps a wolf or other beast. He turned to Hans, opening his mouth to ask if the man felt the feeling too, when he caught the glint of a knife raised in Hans's hands, the sharp tip pointed straight at him. Makellos gasped and stumbled backward a step before he found the smooth rock against his back, trapping him in place like a cornered hare. His heart pounded so loudly in his chest that it drowned out the sounds of the forest, sharpening his vision to only the man before him. "Hans? What...?" The fear that washed through him was unlike anything he had ever felt before, and it choked the rest of the question in his throat.

Makellos could feel heat blazing in his body, his muscles tensed as if to flee, but he couldn't make himself move, only press himself harder against the rock. Hans's shadow loomed over him, blocking out the meager light, and he squeezed his eyes shut, not wanting to see the dagger fall. For a moment, there was silence, and he wondered if the blow had landed, and he had not felt its sting at all. But then he heard a gasping sound from the huntsman, and he peeked one blue eye cautiously open.

"I... I can't do it," Hans said, and the knife fell from his hand to land on the forest floor with a soft thump. A moment later, the man himself also landed on the ground upon his knees, reaching up his gloved hands to grasp at Makellos' cloak. "Forgive me, Your Highness. I beg of you to forgive me."

His breath returned to him in a gasp, and Makellos had to lean back against the large rock, for his knees would not stop shaking. "Hans. I don't understand."

"She's mad. Jealous, because you have grown to be more fair than she. She'll stop at nothing to see you dead." Hans turned his dark eyes up to Makellos. "Run, hide. Leave Falchovari and never return."

Makellos stared down at him, down at this man whom he had known all his life. He didn't need clarification of who "she" was, for he already knew in his heart. His own mother had sent someone to kill him, over something he had not even known. "Go!" Hans said, letting go of Makellos' cloak.

"But... what about you?" Makellos asked. While he did not know the full extent of his mother's cruelty, he was sure that Hans failing to complete the task she had given him would result in something bad happening.

Hans shook his head. "I have served the Queen all of my life. I have watched you grow from a child into a man. A good man. Better than any I have ever known. Whatever the price of my disobedience, I will pay it, because I could not live with myself if I harmed you. I will do my best to hide the truth from her. Please, go. Run away and never come back!"

Makellos turned and began to flee into the trees. He glanced back just once to see Hans still on his knees, immobile as a statue, watching him, his knife still on the ground where he had dropped it. Then he turned back to the dimly lit forest and ran.

He ran as if the very devil were after him, faster than he had ever run in his life. The wind whistled in his ears, "Run! Hide! Run! Hide!" He ducked under tree branches, slipping on roots and bushes, his red cape tangling in a patch of briars. He ripped it free, and the enchanted fabric magically formed itself back together.

He didn't know where he was going or how far he had run. He only knew that he must escape if he wanted to live. He had to find some place where his mother would not find him. Somewhere her eyes could not see and her magic could not reach. Around him, the forest grew darker and darker as the sun sank low in the sky, casting long, grasping shadows that twisted every which way. It was only when he couldn't run any more, when his heart felt like it would explode in his chest and his lungs struggled for every breath, that he finally stopped.

He wasn't sure what direction he was running now, and he could barely see anything. It was possible that in the dim light he could run into a low branch, or fall down a ravine. Or perhaps there were dangerous creatures here who might eat him, or worse, steal his soul. He didn't think he was in the Dark Forest, but he had no way to know what differentiated the Dark Forest from the safer path.

He collapsed down onto the ground, sweat beading on his face and neck, his hands clenching in the leaves under him with a crunch. His eyes grew hot and heavy, and he allowed a few tears to fall. He often cried when he was on his own, but never in front of his mother, for she thought it unbecoming of a man to show such a tender-hearted emotion. He had certainly never seen her cry either. He sat, panting, wiping sweat from his brow and tears from his cheeks with his sleeve, the dampness fading quickly away and leaving his clothing its usual crisp white. He did not have his pack with any of his provisions, and he carried no weapons. He was really and truly alone in the forest.

He wrapped his red cape around himself as his exertion turned itself into an icy chill that sunk beneath his fancy clothes and into his bones. He didn't dare move from his crumpled spot against a large tree, not getting a wink of sleep all night as he stared into the inky darkness.

I t took a long time for the sun to rise high enough above the trees for him to see well enough to stand and search the area around him. He was so tired and cold and thirsty. He realized that he had very few survival skills, having spent most of his life being coddled and provided for in the palace. If he did not find some place to stay, he was guaranteed a much slower death than the blade would have been. Perhaps Hans' mercy had not been a mercy at all.

He turned and headed in the direction he thought was south. He didn't know much about the area beyond Falchovari, but he remembered from his lessons that to the south was a range of mountains and mines where jewels were extracted from the earth.

He came across a hedge of picked-over berries. It was the first edible thing he had seen in the forest that he knew of, so he set about plucking them and eating them as quickly as he could. Thorns scratched his skin, drawing little drops of blood. He wiped them on his shirt, the blood staining it crimson only for a moment before fading away. There were several footprints around the bush of some large animal. Perhaps a wolf or a bear? He had no idea, sure he did not want to encounter the creature, but water had accumulated in the prints. He scooped it out with his hands as best he could, swallowing the mouthfuls even though it gagged him. A prince of the kingdom, reduced to eating half-dead berries off the bush and drinking muddy water. But, he reminded himself, he was alive. And as long as he was alive, he had hope.

Hunger and thirst still clawed at his belly, but it was better than nothing. Perhaps he could distract himself from his discomfort with a song. He had always had a good singing voice, and he thought that maybe the sound of his voice would discourage any larger animals looking to make a morning meal out of him. So, he began to sing, softly at first, then a little louder as the sun warmed his chilled body. And, surprisingly, he did feel better the more he sang.

A soft rustle in the bushes made him jump, his head shooting up as fear filled his heart. Perhaps Hans had gathered his courage and changed his mind, pursuing him into the forest to hunt like a wild stag, easily following the sound of Makellos' voice.

But instead of the dark-haired hunter, a squirrel hopped from the dark leaves. It was a rather large squirrel, a dusky gray color, with big, brown eyes and long whiskers. It tipped its head curiously at him, standing up on its hind feet, its tiny front paws up in front of it.

"Oh! Hello, little one," Makellos said gently, lowering himself to one knee to look less foreboding. "Are you lost too?"

The squirrel tipped its head again before drifting to closer to him, its little nose quivering. Its eyes were wide, but it showed no fear as it approached.

"I don't suppose you are lost the same way I am," Makellos said. "This is your home, after all. You are quite a fine little fellow. You must be quite clever to have survived this long and grown so big."

The squirrel continued to slowly walk toward him on his four little paws, almost silent over the forest floor, until he stopped right by the prince's boot, staring up at him. Makellos gave him a small smile. He figured that being a squirrel must be much simpler than being a man, though he was sure the danger was greater for something so small and wild. "I am Makellos," he said, giving the squirrel a nod. The squirrel's fluffy tail snapped in what seemed to be acknowledgement. "I feel rather bad that I do not know your name," Makellos said. "Perhaps I could give you one?"

The squirrel's nose twitched.

"May I call you Buschig? For your bushy tail?"

The little nose twitched again.

"A pleasure then to meet you, Herr Buschig," Makellos said, giving him a polite bow of his head.

Buschig stared back at him before bobbing his own tiny, pointed head a few times in return. Evidently, the introduction pleased him. Makellos smiled in delight. It was nice to have a friend here.

"I don't know what to do. I'm all alone out here. I have always had servants to take care of my needs. I'm afraid I don't know the first thing about surviving in a forest like you. Would you know of somewhere I can go?"

Buschig cocked his head to one side, nose twitching, before he turned and scampered into the trees. Makellos watched him go, still kneeling on the cool ground. The squirrel had almost darted out of sight before he turned around, looked straight at Makellos, and came scurrying back. He stopped by his boot again, sitting up on his hind legs, and began to chitter at him.

"Oh, do you want me to follow you?" Makellos asked.

Buschig turned and scampered a few paces, then turned back to look at him. Makellos got to his feet, brushing off the leaves that stuck to him, the dirt fading away. He began to follow after the squirrel, who ran ahead a few dozen paces, then stopped and turned to wait for him to catch up before hurrying on ahead again. Makellos followed the squirrel through the dense underbrush. Buschig was fast, but he always stopped and waited for Makellos to catch up before dashing ahead again.

The prince was starting to see more wildlife again too. Birds twittered in the trees, echoing back the sound when he whistled at them. Rabbits poked twitchy noses out of bushes. Other squirrels and chipmunks dashed about, chasing one another through the trees. He even saw a doe and her fawn sliding through the trees a little way off. Any time he sang a few notes, the creatures would stop and stare at him. A few joined Buschig in leading the way through the forest, giving Makellos an even easier lead to follow.

They continued this walk for most of the day before they came within sight of a creek. The sun was sinking again when Buschig suddenly ran around a large tree and disappeared from sight as the other animals dispersed into the nearby foliage. Makellos followed after Buschig and discovered that the roots of the tree formed a little covered hollow in the earth. Buschig sat inside the little cavern, chittering softly. Next to him was another large squirrel and three smaller squirrels whose eyes were not open and whose fur was only starting to grow in. Makellos knelt down to peer into the root hollow and smiled. "Is this your family?" he asked Buschig.

Buschig flipped his tail and made some soft noises. Makellos bowed his head at the other squirrel. "Hello, Frau Buschig. Your babies are beautiful."

The female squirrel chattered, then picked up her babies one by one and carried them back into the far corner of the hollow. It was cool and slightly damp, smelling of rich earth and autumn leaves. "Thank you so very much." Buschig squeaked and snapped his tail again before he trotted over to join his family at the back of the root hollow.

Makellos drank his fill of water from the creek and stripped off his clothes to wash himself. It was very cold, but he felt better being clean again. He then curled up in the dimness of the little den and gave the family of squirrels a grateful smile. He wrapped his cloak around him as best he could, and, using his arm for a pillow, closed his eyes. Within moments, he was fast asleep.

Four

When he awoke the next morning, the largest squirrel sat at the entrance of the little cavern, as if standing guard. Makellos gave him a smile. "Good morning, Herr Buschig." He sat up, brushing off his clothes that still looked completely immaculate, despite having slept all night in them on the ground. He glanced down to find that there was a pile of berries, mushrooms, and nuts sitting on a leaf nearby. "Is this for me?" he asked.

Buschig twitched his tail.

"Thank you," Makellos said, taking one of the berries and popping it into his mouth. It was fat and sweet, as good as anything he had eaten in the palace. Of course, the animals would know where to find the best fruit in the forest, even in the midst of a famine. He ate everything in the little pile except for one large berry, which he offered to Frau Buschig who lay on her side at the back of the hollow, her three babies nursing. She took it in her little scratchy paws and nibbled on it gratefully.

Makellos turned to the father squirrel with another grateful smile. "Thank you for inviting me into your home and taking care of me, Herr Buschig. But I can't stay here forever. Do you know if there's somewhere in the forest I can go? Or the mountains?"

Buschig chattered, his little whiskers quivering, and he gave a little scamper into the woods before coming back, as he had yesterday. Makellos bid goodbye to Frau Buschig and the babies before crawling out of the little hollow and rising to his feet. He stretched as best he could. He was unaccustomed to lying on the ground, and his whole body ached from the coolness of the night and the hardness of the earth, but he was still alive. He turned and followed Buschig into the trees. So far, the kindly squirrel had not steered him wrong.

They walked for a while, stopping a few times when they found water for Makellos to quench his thirst. The sun was hot overhead, though the trees offered ample shade. They really were quite beautiful, with their radiant halos of reds and oranges and yellows. And when he sang again, animals poked their heads out of trees and burrows and dens to listen. The forest was alive with life, and he was too. He felt so much more positive that he could make it through this trial. The thought of leaving Falchovari, the only home he had ever known, pained him deep inside. He had barely been able to see any of it and meet its people, but what he had seen on his brief travels was enough for him to know that the kingdom was in trouble. The famine was making everyone suffer. He couldn't blame the people for being angry. The Queen had done nothing to ensure that her subjects were taken care of. They were poor and hungry and lost, just like he was now, with no hope of a better life. He wished there was something more he could do. He was a prince, but he had never been allowed to do anything helpful.

He was so lost in his own thoughts that he nearly tripped over Buschig when the squirrel came to an abrupt halt. Buschig chattered at him, his quivery nose pointed ahead. Makellos could see what looked like a sunny clearing in the trees, and he hurried up his steps as Buschig scampered toward it. When he stepped through the tree line, the sight that greeted him was most welcome. It was a quaint little single-story cottage. The walls were made of a combination of wood and stone, the roof thatched with straw and water reeds. There was a well out front, and the windows appeared to be patterned glass. Off to the side of the house was a little garden patch. Makellos drew closer to inspect it. Weeds grew out of control over the plants within, so much so that it was difficult to see where weed ended and sprouted vegetable began. The few vegetables he spotted were not as big and plump as the vegetables he was used to seeing on the table at the palace. His stomach growled in hunger, and he reached to take several small tomatoes off the vine to eat. He felt ashamed at not asking permission first, but hopefully he could offer a trinket or service to make up for his wild breach of etiquette.

There was no sound from the house, and no smoke emerged from the stone chimney. Curious, he moved back around to the front of the house. The front door was made of heavy slabs of wood, but it stood slightly ajar. This far into the woods, perhaps there was no fear of thieves. Makellos peered inside but could see nothing in the dimness. He rapped his knuckles lightly upon the door. "Hello? Is there anyone at home?"

He waited for a moment, but only the silence of the forest answered him. He knocked again, but there was no movement from within. He hated to intrude, but the door *was* open. Perhaps no one lived here any longer. He pushed the door open wider. Its hinges gave a rusty creak that sounded much too loud in the stillness. The lintel of the doorframe was right about the height of his head. Makellos was not a particularly tall fellow, and the doors at the palace were quite tall and grand. Was that how peasant dwellings were built? To conserve heat, perhaps? He ducked his head to enter the little cottage.

Inside, it was quite dim. Makellos had to squint to see into its dusky interior. Patches of forest sunlight slanted through in several places, and Makellos realized as he looked up that the thatching in the roof had worn away, leaving several holes that showed the sky above.

The space that he entered was a large single room, with a long table and benches laid out in the center of it, upon which sat many pewter cups, plates, and silverware, still sporting a few crumbs. There was a large stone fireplace and hearth that was currently unlit. There was a washtub with a pump, and various nooks and crannies stuffed with all manner of things needed for habitation. A clothesline was run between two beams, and several bedraggled-looking shirts and trousers hung from it. There was a single door off to the left that was closed tightly. Leading to a bedroom and washroom, Makellos guessed. The few pieces of furniture in this area were tattered and in various states of disrepair. The room smelled of dust and clothing that needed a wash. But it did not seem as though it had been abandoned. Someone was living here, perhaps currently out cutting wood or bringing things to market.

He didn't wish to intrude, but this was the only house he had seen since he had entered the forest; he might wander for days without finding another. He would stay until the owner returned home, beg a reprieve for the night, and then would continue south in the morning.

He glanced back to see Buschig sitting on the doorstep, giving him a hopeful look. Makellos gave him a deep bow. "Thank you, Herr Buschig. I am forever in your debt for your kindness." The squirrel bowed his head in return, then turned and scampered back into the forest to return to his family.

Makellos spotted a lantern hanging near the door with some striking sticks to light it. The front window was close to it, feeble light attempting to make its way through the glass. He realized as he approached it that the windows were not actually stained glass; they were just so covered in grime that the sun couldn't reach through. "Well, that won't do," he said out loud to himself. He pulled his sleeve down over his hand and used it to wipe away the layers of dirt from one corner of the glass. A shaft of early afternoon sunlight slanted through the spot, and his sleeve was none the worse for wear with its enchantment.

"I can wash the windows," he said out loud to no one in particular, but it was a little more reassuring than the silence of the empty cottage and surrounding forest. He might as well make himself useful while he waited for the occupant.

He went to the pump and washtub. The tub was filled with all manner of dirty dishes and cooking utensils. He would wash those as well, once the windows were clean enough to offer him better light. He filled a bucket with water from the pump that gushed cheerfully, then found a pile of rags. He set about to washing the windows, first from the inside, then from the outside. There was something very satisfactory about removing the layers of grime and dirt from the window panes, leaving them clear and sparkling, catching the warm sunlight.

Once all of the windows that showed into the main room were clean, he returned to find the inside much improved by the light. Dust caught the sun and glimmered in the air like diamonds, but the place did seem to be quite cozy. He was getting warm in his royal clothing, so Makellos decided to take off the blue tunic and red cape he wore and rolled his shirtsleeves up past his elbows. He so rarely was in such a disheveled state of undress, but he had seen many of the stable hands dress this way, and he realized he found it quite freeing. Being able to move without the restriction of the pompous clothing was a relief.

He left the door open to catch the afternoon breeze as he set about to washing the pile of dishes in the washtub, followed by the ones on the table. He stacked them neatly to dry. His hands were beginning to prune; oh, how his mother would scold him if she saw him now!

There was a large cast iron cauldron near the fireplace. It looked as though it hadn't been washed in a year. He knew from his many adventures in the palace kitchen how important a cauldron could be for cooking and heating water. He worried he wouldn't be able to lift it if it was filled to the brim with water, as it was quite large, so he drew himself another bucket of water, grabbed a sliver of soap, and moved over to the cauldron. He tipped it carefully on its side, making sure it was not going to roll anywhere, before he got down on his knees, dipped a rag in the water, and began to wash.

After a few minutes, Makellos began to sing as he scrubbed the inside of the large cauldron. The reflection of his voice off of its heavy metal interior was oddly fascinating. It certainly beat the silence around him. He let out an experimental whistle, delighting in the way the high note pinged off the metal and fluttered about his head like a butterfly. The Queen had always discouraged him from whistling; it was unbecoming of a prince, and it would create wrinkles around his lips. He wasn't sure why that would be a concern. He was young, and even still, wrinkles were just a part of life. Whistling was quite fun, just another way to make music. And the sound echoing inside the cauldron made him laugh. He couldn't remember the last time he had laughed.

He slid back out of the cauldron, swiping his ebony hair out of his eyes with his forearm before he froze. He was not alone. Someone was standing in the open doorway of the cottage. It took Makellos a moment to make out the details of the figure silhouetted there. He was dressed in tattered clothes that looked to be more patches than actual clothing. He had protruding ears, big blue eyes, and a shock of bright red hair. At first, Makellos thought the person to be a child, for his stature was much shorter than his own. But, the prince realized, the person's face was much older than a child's, though his cheeks were bare and soft. And his proportions were strange. His head seemed a little larger than it should be, and his arms and legs were shorter and thinner, giving his torso a rather blocky look, despite the fact that he was nearly as thin as the prince.

The two stared at one another for a moment before Makellos realized that this must be the person who lived in this cottage, and he had just come home to find a stranger on his knees, scrubbing the pots and pans. He gave the young man a smile, the friendliest he could, pushing himself to his feet, his back giving a little protest at the change in position. The red-haired man in the doorway backed up a step, and Makellos held out his hands quickly from his side. "I'm sorry if I startled you," he said quickly. "I'm unarmed, I mean you no harm."

The young man's shoulders were clenched and slightly turned away from him, as if expecting a blow. No doubt he did not receive many visitors this far into the wilder parts of Falchovari. Makellos kept his polite smile in place. "I'm very sorry. I was lost in the woods, and I needed a place to stay." If he had had any money, he would have offered it.

The young man slowly turned toward him again. Makellos could see that over his shoulder he had a rope, in which was tied a bony dead hare and a scrawny-looking pheasant. It appeared that the young man had been out hunting for a meal. He had a bow strapped to his back. But he made no move to grab it, only continued to stare at him.

Makellos wondered if it was wise to give the young man his real name or not. Despite the fact that the Queen ruled the kingdom, he was still a descendent of hers and therefore might be seen as being partially responsible for the troubles of the peasantry. But on the other hand, he thought, if he was truthful about who he was and why he was in this stranger's house, perhaps the young man would be understanding and appreciative of his honesty. He took a slow step, keeping his hands out. "My name is Makellos."

No recognition flickered in the young man's eyes. Perhaps he did not know the name of the prince who lived so far north of him. Makellos took several more steps. The young man did not cower again, though he made no move to approach him either. Now that they were closer, he could see that the man was probably a handful of winters older than his own twenty, despite his small stature.

"Do you live here?" Makellos asked, gesturing a hand around him to the humble abode.

The young man nodded slowly. Makellos gave him a friendly smile. "Is it just you alone here?"

The young man hesitated for a moment, then shook his head. "Who else lives here?" Makellos asked politely.

After a moment, the young man held up a hand, splaying five stubby fingers, then his other hand with two. Makellos blinked. "Seven of you?" The young man nodded. "Goodness, it must be quite crowded," Makellos said with a slight frown, gazing around at the singular living space. "I suppose it might be an imposition then for me to ask to stay the night?"

The young man looked thoughtful, then shrugged and gestured to the empty room. "You need to discuss it with the others who live here?" Makellos guessed, and the pink-cheeked man nodded. "That is entirely fair," Makellos said, giving him a polite smile. "Would you prefer if I leave until they return?"

The redhead shook his head quickly and gave Makellos a hint of a smile, shy and sweet. He held up the pheasant and hare, then motioned to the large cauldron that Makellos had been scrubbing. "Those are for your dinner?" Makellos asked, and the little man nodded again. "I may not look like it, but I am actually quite good in the kitchen," Makellos said. "If you'd like, I'd be happy to prepare them for you."

The man's smile brightened, and he finally stepped inside the little house. He pointed to himself and the animals over his shoulder, making a chopping motion with his hands. "You can dress the meat?" The young man nodded. Makellos felt relief flood over him, glad he would not have to butcher the animals himself. He had done it a few times in the castle kitchens in his years of experimenting and learning, but it had always made him quite sad. He was happy that he was not expected to take on the gruesome task now. "I will go pick some vegetables while you do that," he offered, and the man's blue eyes shone with delight. He gestured at a nearby basket, which Makellos happily took and headed out the door and around to the garden.

The garden patch was actually larger than he had first realized, but he supposed it would have to be if there were seven people living in this little house. The red-haired young man had not said a word to him yet; perhaps he was mute. Makellos wondered if that would be the case with everyone who lived in the house. Was it a family who lived here? Would he be able to communicate with them? Would they know how to read or write? He knew some peasants had that education, but certainly not all.

Makellos wondered all of this to himself as he walked through the garden, pulling fresh carrots and potatoes from the ground and dusting them carefully off. They were not as large as the ones he saw in the palace, but the fact that this home had its own garden at all here in the woods was extremely beneficial. There were a few sprigs of herbs growing here and there as well, so he added a few to his basket. The garden could do with some weeding and pruning, but it could be quite lovely and bountiful with some tender loving care.

He headed back inside the coolness of the cottage. The red-haired young man was in the corner, meat laid out on a slab of wood. Makellos could see the feathers from the pheasant in another basket nearby, and the rabbit pelt off to the side. It seemed like nothing would go to waste. Makellos set firewood inside of the hearth and attempted to light it, but he had never lit a fire before, and he felt the little man's eyes on him as he did. He looked up sheepishly as the redhead approached him. "I am not used to doing this."

The young man smiled, letting out a soft breath that sounded like a chuckle. He picked up the tinder box, showing Makellos the steel and flint within, and then struck it several times to produce a spark. It caught the bundle of dry grass the young man held, and then he set it into the hearth and blew on it. The sparks flared, and a small fire began to glow deep within. Makellos clapped his hands with delight. "Thank you! I shall have to practice doing that myself sometime."

The red-haired man let out another airy-sounding laugh before he got up and went back to his work. Makellos finished scrubbing the large cauldron. Once it was done, the young man returned to his side and helped him set it upright and hang it on the hook over the fire that was crackling pleasantly now. Makellos filled the kettle with water from the pump multiple times to make the base of the soup. He took the prepared meat and put it into the pot, since that would take longer to cook. He was aware that the little redhead kept an eye on him as he worked. The man grabbed a washboard and a basket of clothes. He held them up for Makellos to see and inclined his head to the door. "You're going outside to wash clothes?" Makellos asked, and the young man nodded with a bright smile. "That sounds good, I will prep the rest of dinner and get the dishes ready." He moved over to wash and cut the vegetables as the young man walked out into the fading sunshine.

He wondered about the other occupants of the house as he laid out place settings for eight on the large wooden table. He knew it was presumptuous of him to assume he could at least stay for dinner, but hopefully they would not turn him out without at least a bite to eat. Fruits and nuts could only sustain him for so long, and with the weather getting colder, they would become more difficult for him to find. He couldn't rely on the generosity of the forest animals forever either.

He dumped the vegetables into the simmering pot, adding several handfuls of fresh herbs and some salt from a jar to the mixture, and then put the lid onto the large cauldron. He washed the dishes he had used and put the excess peelings and roots of vegetables in the basket to take out to the garden later to scatter. He had never learned how to grow his own vegetables and herbs, but he did remember Auntie Anne telling him that he could do that when he had leftover bits. Especially with food being so scarce throughout the kingdom, it would not do to be wasteful.

Five

The sunlight had nearly disappeared behind the trees when the young man entered again, his tunic wet from doing the laundry. Makellos could barely see it hanging on a clothes line outside in the fading light. He lifted up the lid from the cauldron, hand wrapped in a rag, giving the soup a stir. The young man inhaled greedily, and Makellos could practically see his mouth water. He laughed. "When can we expect everyone to return?"

The young man blinked, then cocked his head to the side, as if listening. After a moment, he pointed out the open door, a large smile splitting his face. Makellos listened too. At first, he heard nothing. Then, slowly in the distance, he heard the tramp of feet through the forest, crunching leaves and evergreen needles underfoot, and the soft murmur of voices. He turned to the redheaded young man. "Is that them?"

The young man nodded, giving him a hopeful smile.

Makellos took a deep breath. If these new people didn't want him to stay in their house, he would soon have to brave the forest again. The voices were getting louder and clearer now, and then a group of people broke through the tree line. They were all bunched together but formed a single-file line as they approached the house. The redhead made a motion for Makellos to stay where he was before stepping around him to stand in the cottage's doorway. He waved his hands and made a few gestures toward the voices. "Someone's here?" he heard a voice say, followed by an unclear babble of voices behind it. The redhead stepped aside.

Someone entered the hut, then stopped short, causing the others behind him to collide with him in a heap on the doorstep. There were several shouts and a few curses from the group, and a shove that sent the man in front inside several more steps.

The gathering at the door was unlike any Makellos had ever seen. There were six men, of various ages and shapes. He was sure he was staring at them as much as they were staring at him. He could almost hear the scolding from his mother and his tutors that it was rude to gape, but he could hardly help himself. The six men were of varying heights, but heights that he had only ever seen in children. The tallest one, the one who had stopped short in the doorway, was at least a foot shorter than Makellos, not even reaching his shoulder. He had a pair of round glass spectacles balanced a little precariously on his slightly wide nose, his bushy muttonchops quivering slightly. Behind the man with the glasses were two men about the same height as each other who looked like they were probably brothers. Each had slicked back chestnut-colored hair and thick eyebrows over identical hazel eyes, though one had a pointed goatee and the other only had a few days of stubble on his cheeks.

Makellos gave them a polite smile and a small bow. "Hello."

"You're the prince." The warm voice came from a man just behind the spectacled one, with a thick beard but no moustache. When he stepped out, Makellos could see that his body was quite rotund, but his head seemed larger, and his arms and legs were much smaller in proportion to the rest of him.

Whispers and murmurs ran through the group, and Makellos gave a small nod. "Yes, I am," he said softly.

"Prince Makellos?" asked another voice. It took a moment for him to find the speaker, for he was the smallest person Makellos had ever seen. The top of his head only reached as far as Makellos' waist. He had a large forehead, brown eyes peering out from beneath it. Makellos might have mistaken him for a child if it wasn't for the fact that he was balding and had a thick, fluffy moustache and beard, all of which were streaked with gray.

"What are you doing here?" demanded a different voice. The chestnut-haired brothers parted to let through another man whose arms seemed too long for his blocky torso. His voice was as sharp as the salt-and-pepper beard on his chin, his dark brown eyes boring into Makellos like an auger into a tree, despite the fact that he only came up to Makellos' elbow.

Makellos gave them another small bow. "I'm so very sorry to intrude on your home."

"We don't know why he's here," said the sharp man, turning to the others around him as if Makellos had not spoken at all. "Find out what he's doing in our house."

"Oh, uh, yes, what are you and who are you doing?" asked the bespectacled man, turning back to Makellos as he tried to sound huffy and stern, chest puffed up like a rooster. The two chestnut-haired men behind him laughed heartily, and Makellos' lips curved into a smile.

The one with the pointed beard rubbed his eyes with his hand, as if in pain, before shooting the spectacled man a pointed look. "Tell him he ain't welcome here, Der."

The man called Der looked at the sharp man with confusion. "Why would he not be welcome?"

"You think the son of *Her Majesty*," the man said the words so sarcastically that Makellos could feel the sourness in his own mouth, "is here because of something good for all of us?"

Though he didn't know why, Makellos had a feeling that these men were no friend to his family. But they already knew who he was and had not attacked him or thrown him out yet, which was certainly a good first step.

"Please," he said softly, bowing his head. "My mother, the Queen, tried to have me killed. I ran away, and I need a place to stay."

There were quiet gasps all around. "Why?" asked the brother with the stubbled cheeks.

Makellos didn't have it in his heart to make up a lie. "My mother has always been the fairest in the kingdom, up until now. But she has deemed me to be more fair than she, and she cannot abide that."

He lifted his head to see a few of the short men blushing and realized they were all assessing his features. That felt rather strange, to know that one was being stared at only for their fairness, but he hoped that it might help them understand his predicament.

"You *are* very fair," said the rotund man.

"Thank you," Makellos said with a sweet smile. "Might I know your names?"

The dark-eyed man with the pointed beard let out a ha-rumph, but everyone else in the room ignored him.

"My name is Der," said the bespectacled man. "You've already met Dagobert." He nodded to the red-haired young man that Makellos had been working with all afternoon.

"Ah. A pleasure to finally make your acquaintance, Herr Dagobert," Makellos said, giving him a polite bow. Dagobert's cheeks went pink, and he dipped his head slightly in return.

"This is Hardwic," Der said, motioning to the round man with the shorter limbs.

"Hello, I'm Hardwic!" the man sang out cheerfully, his nearly all-white beard bobbing. "Happy to meet you, your highness."

"The pleasure is mine," Makellos said, his heart warming at the brightness from the man.

"And Sigurd, and Sigmund." Der pointed to the two men with the chestnut hair.

"I'm the older one," said Sigurd, the one with the stubble on his cheeks.

"He was the trial run. I got all the improvements," said Sigmund with a smirk on his bearded face.

Makellos laughed as Sigurd gave his brother a punch on the arm. "I'm two inches taller than you."

"Yes, because those extra two inches went somewhere else on me," Sigmund said with an equally smug look. Makellos felt his cheeks go red, and he pressed his lips together to keep from laughing aloud.

"Now now," scolded Der, his bushy brows knitting together like he was scolding two unruly schoolboys. "Let's be appropriate in front of the prince."

"Sorry," Sigurd grumbled.

"He's sorry," Sigmund said, giving his older brother an elbow to the ribs.

Der rolled his eyes, then motioned to the shortest member of their group. "This is Bernhardt."

The little man with the balding head nodded politely. He seemed to be entirely proportionate other than a slightly larger forehead, though he was only half the size of the men Makellos had known.

Der turned to the last person in their group, the man with the sharp beard and dark eyes. "And Grimwald."

"Pleased to meet you," Makellos said, giving the man a bow. Grimwald just glared back at him. They were the strangest bunch of people he had ever seen. The tallest of them, Der with the spectacles, only stood as tall as his biceps, down to the smallest one, Bernhardt, who didn't even come up to his waist. The only people he had ever seen at such heights were children, but these were definitely not children, even Dagobert who was obviously the youngest one of the group. A few of them were more proportional, but some of them had heads that seemed a little too big, limbs that seemed a bit too long or a bit too short, or torsos that were blockier than what he was used to seeing. Most of them seemed of older middle age, with gray at their temples or in their facial hair, though he thought Dagobert to be less than thirty winters old.

"I am very pleased to make your acquaintance," Makellos said, giving them all one more bow. It was better to be overly polite than to accidentally be rude. A sudden waft of scent came over him, and he could tell the others smelled it too; the comforting aroma of the soup in the cauldron. "I hope you do not mind that I borrowed your kitchen. The soup should be ready."

"You made us soup?" cried out Hardwic in excitement. "It smells delightful, your highness!"

"Oh, please, call me Makellos," the prince said, holding up his hands with a sheepish smile. "No need to stand on ceremony when I am the one seeking your favor."

"Aw, he's so cute, let's keep him," said the brother with the beard on his chin.

"He's not a pet, Sigmund," scolded Bernhardt.

"I know it is a great imposition on you and your home," Makellos tried again. "I do not expect to stay here without earning my keep."

"There, you see?" said Sigmund with a slightly smug look.

"And what use is a pampered little princeling to us?" Grimwald asked, giving Makellos a glower.

"Now now," Der said again, shaking his finger at Grimwald. "He has already made us supper. The least we can do is discuss it."

"Please, let us sit and dine. You all have worked so hard today, I am sure you must be exhausted," Makellos said, gesturing to the table. "No one should have serious discussions on an empty stomach."

There was a rumble of agreement between the little men. Bags were set down, hands were washed at the pump, and a loaf of bread was produced from one of the bags and set upon the table. Everyone sat on the benches, which Makellos realized were built much higher than what he was used to, likely to help the short men reach the tabletop easier. He ladled soup from the cauldron into bowls, setting one before each of them. Grimwald lifted his spoon to dig in, but a scolding click of the tongue from Bernhardt stopped him, and Grimwald sat back with folded arms and a grumpy look upon his face until Makellos had served bowls to everyone and one for himself. He sat down on the end of one bench next to Dagobert, finding it slightly awkward for his own taller frame. He gestured to the table with a bright smile. "Please, eat."

Grimwald was the first to pick up his spoon and shove a bite into his mouth. It must have been very hot, but he swallowed it without a sign of discomfort, ignoring Makellos entirely. The others picked up their spoons, blowing onto the bite or into their bowls to cool it, except Der, who sliced the loaf of bread and passed it around the table, starting with Makellos. Makellos took a single slice, and the plate went around the table, until it came to Dagobert on his right. The plate was empty. Der put up a hand to his mouth. "Oh dear, I'm so used to cutting for seven. I'm so sorry."

"It's all right," Makellos replied with a smile, taking his own slice of bread and ripping it in half, holding it out to Dagobert. The redhead took it with a bright smile, mouthing 'thank you.'

There were sounds of appreciation all around the table as the little men ate. Makellos was happy with the way the soup turned out, considering the limits he was working with in this cozy cottage, rather than the overabundant larders of the palace. He offered seconds, and everyone gratefully accepted, even Grimwald, who held out his bowl begrudgingly.

Sharing a table with so many people was rather nice, Makellos thought. He had almost always eaten alone or just with his mother, and their conversations were often spent with Queen Schön critiquing him or telling him how he could be better, be more perfect as a prince. The contented silence was a nice change. Once everyone had eaten their fill, Makellos asked, "May I enquire how all of you came to live here together?"

There were glances all around the table, and Makellos had a feeling that the topic was a sore spot amongst them. But Der cleared his throat and spoke up.

"Many years ago," he began, "the Queen decided that she only wanted perfection amongst the people in her kingdom. So, anyone that did not meet her standards were rounded up. Little people like us, and people who might have looked or acted differently."

Makellos had never heard of such a thing happening; it must have been before he was born, he thought, which perhaps explained why he had not seen anyone that did not look out of the ordinary around the palace.

"Most of us lost our livelihoods," Sigurd said, staring down at his empty bowl. "Our homes, our families, gone. We," he lifted his head to include the others around the table with a nod of his head, "were banished to the mines to work. Away from the Queen's gaze."

"What happened to your families?" Makellos asked, his eyes wide. "Your sisters, your wives, your children?"

An uncomfortable silence fell between all of the little men, feet shuffling, eyes averted. Only Grimwald seemed able to meet his gaze, his dark brown eyes hard as stone, his arms crossed over his chest. "The Queen had them killed. So they could not bear any children who might end up small like them. Or like their fathers." He glanced side to side to encompass the other men in the room.

Makellos' heart leapt into his throat, choking him as it beat an erratic rhythm. Everything suddenly felt so dark and small. His own body felt too tight for the emotions that welled within him. He set down his spoon as his hands began to tremble. Dagobert reached over and placed a hand lightly on top of one of Makellos', giving it a gentle squeeze. "I... I never knew," he said softly, heat gathering behind his eyes.

Grimwald snorted, but Der and the others looked at him with various levels of sympathy. "It was a long time ago," Der said. "There were more of us back then. More outcasts, that is. Some have died since then. As far as we know, we are the only ones left. So, we banded together and have lived here for years."

Makellos gulped a breath, quickly wiping at his eyes with his handkerchief. "I am so very sorry. If I had known..."

"If you had known, what?" Grimwald asked, gazing sternly at Makellos across the table. "What would a spoiled brat like you have done against your own mother?"

"Now, Grim, that's not fair," said Hardwic. "The prince has given no indication of being a spoiled brat. And he's in just as much danger from the Queen as we were."

Grimwald glowered but lowered his eyes to his soup bowl again.

Makellos smiled weakly. "I do not know what I would have done, or what I could even do. My mother rules the kingdom, not I. But what was done to you all is horrific, and I would not ever be a part of such cruelty."

Dagobert smiled and squeezed Makellos' wrist again.

"You seem like a kind soul," said Bernhardt, taking a sip from his mug of water. "Very unlike the Queen."

"That is perhaps the best compliment I could have received," Makellos said, perking up a little, his eyes and smile growing a bit brighter. "Thank you, Bernhardt." The little man nodded in return. "So, you all live here together in the forest. What do you do?"

"We work in the mountain mines, not far from here," Hardwic said, gesturing with his spoon toward the forest out the window. "Every day, six of us are required to report to work. So, we rotate each day who stays home. That one takes care of the house and does the hunting and whatnot."

Makellos stared around in surprise. "That is certainly a lot of work for one person to do alone," he said. It also explained the decrepit state of the roof and the garden. How could anyone be expected to clean, hunt, cook enough food for seven, wash and dry clothes, tend the garden, chop wood, and keep the house in repair with only one day off each week after six days of hard labor?

"But now that you're here, we have an extra pair of hands!" Sigmund said.

"We need the help," Sigurd added. "Winter is coming, and we have very little time left to prep for the cold months."

"We need lots more firewood," Der said. "We will need as much as we can cut, and probably more than that. And food preserved for when the game is scarce and the garden is covered in snow."

"Do you still work in the mines even in the dead of winter?" Makellos asked.

"Oh yes, every day," Bernhardt said gravely. "If we don't, the guards have the authority to place us under arrest. Which would then mean taking us to the palace to face the Queen."

"As far as we know, she's all but forgotten about us," Der said, taking his spectacles off his nose and wiping at them with a pocket handkerchief that was more holes than handkerchief.

"What do you do in the mines?" Makellos asked.

"The mine is full of jewels," said Sigurd and Sigmund at the same time, and they elbowed each other playfully before Sigurd continued. "But we don't know what we dig them for. They get taken away to the palace."

Makellos had a sinking feeling in his stomach. "I know what they are used for," he said softly. "My mother loves jewelry, but even more than that, her magic is powered by jewels."

"What sort of magic?" asked Hardwic curiously.

"I don't really know everything she is capable of," Makellos admitted. "She has never taught me any magic, if I even have any at all. But I do know that she uses the jewels to create the elixir she drinks every day. It keeps her from aging, keeps her beautiful."

"And yet, for all her magic, she is still not as beautiful as you," said Sigmund with a flirty bat of his lashes.

Makellos laughed a little at that. "I am sure it was quite the shock to her."

"Well, I think we understand why you ran away," Der said with a glance around the table to encompass all of them. "What sort of skills do you have?"

"Oh, yes, of course. I love to cook and bake," Makellos said thoughtfully. "I admit that I am not overly familiar with most of the work involved with running a home, but I am a fast learner, and I am very willing to earn my keep."

"Like we said, even just having an extra pair of hands to help while we prep for winter would be most appreciated," Hardwic said hopefully. "I think he should stay."

"And what happens when the Queen finds out he's still alive?" Grimwald suddenly piped up. "If she tried to kill him before, you think she'll stop now?"

"But she doesn't know where I am," Makellos said. "To be truthful, even *I* don't know exactly where I am."

"I'm certain she will find out eventually," Bernhardt said, looking apologetic at the thought. "The old Queen's a sly one. But the woods are vast, and there are any number of dangers, especially if she thinks that perhaps he stumbled into the Dark Forest. Winter is coming on soon, we can't expect him to survive in the forest alone."

"May I offer a suggestion?" Makellos asked timidly, not sure if he should speak out of turn, but every pair of eyes turned expectantly to him, so he continued. "You obviously need help here in preparation for the cold. Let me stay with you and help you through the winter, and then, come spring, I can continue my travels south over the mountains."

"I think that's a marvelous idea!" said Hardwic, giving Makellos a rosy-cheeked smile.

"As do I," Der said. "All in favor, raise your hand?"

Six hands went up around the table. Grimwald's stayed firmly crossed under his armpit.

"Well, it's six to one," Der said brightly. "It is decided, the prince shall stay with us."

Whoops and cheers went up from the others, and Dagobert gave Makellos' wrist another loving press.

"We need to be extra careful though," Hardwic said suddenly. "We can't just talk openly about the prince of Falchovari living in our house."

Grimwald let out a derisive snort that everyone else ignored.

"Perhaps a different name?" Bernhardt suggested. "Call him something else when there is the risk of anyone hearing?"

Several of the men nodded. "So, what do we call him?" Der asked. A soft rustle went through the room, a few mutters and mumbles.

Makellos almost jumped in surprise when a hand next to him went up. It was Dagobert. The room went oddly silent, everyone looking at the young man in curious anticipation. Dagobert looked around, his blue eyes wide, his cheeks bright pink. He swallowed hard, his Adam's apple bobbing, before he looked adoringly up at Makellos. He reached his hand over to run his fingers shyly over the crisp white sleeve of Makellos' shirtsleeves. "Snow. Snow White," he said, his voice soft but sweet and clear.

There was a collective intake of breath around the room from the little men, followed by all eyes turning to Makellos in expectation. Makellos smiled, reaching a hand up to stroke over Dagobert's fingers on his sleeve. "I like it," he said.

"Well, if his highness likes it, then Snow White it shall be," Der said with another bright smile, giving Dagobert an affectionate look.

Grimwald snorted softly and mumbled something about "ridiculous name" under his breath, but everyone else ignored him.

Dagobert shifted over toward Makellos, who leaned over as well, thinking that the young man was about to whisper something in his ear. But instead, he felt the soft brush of lips on his cheek. Dagobert pulled back quickly after that, his face completely red with embarrassment. Makellos blinked in surprise, then smiled kindly at Dagobert and placed his other hand over his to give his stubby fingers a gentle squeeze. "Thank you." Dagobert flushed, a large, dopey smile on his face as he gazed adoringly at Makellos.

After that, the group broke up into several smaller ones to handle evening chores in the light from the lanterns on the wall and the fire in the hearth, for the outside had grown menacingly dark once more. Makellos found himself with Hardwic, washing dishes at the pump. "Is Dagobert usually mute?" Makellos asked softly. "He didn't say a word to me when we were here this afternoon."

Hardwic chuckled softly. "He can speak. But he rarely does."

"Why?" Makellos asked.

"Well..." Hardwic looked thoughtful. "We're not fully sure. He tends to only speak when something is very important to him, and then only a few words, as you saw. He was quite young when the Queen rounded us up, so he has spent most of his life in the mines."

"How awful," Makellos said softly.

Hardwick nodded, his mouth set in a surprisingly grim line compared to his normally cheerful demeanor. "He was the only small person in his family. We never learned what happened to them after he was taken away. Perhaps they still live, or perhaps they were sent into exile or imprisoned. Or..." Hardwic let the last possibility hang in the air between them like a soap bubble.

Makellos shuddered. "My mother is cruel," he said, lowering his eyes to the soapy water. "I am ashamed to be her son."

Hardwic gave him a gentle pat on the small of his back, the highest his smaller arms could reach. "We don't choose our parents," he said. "But we can choose our families."

Makellos smiled a bit at the words. It was true. His mother had birthed him, but she was hardly what he considered his 'family.' "Did you have a family, Hardwic?"

"I did," the round man said, his voice dropping a little. "A wife and a little girl. All of us touched by the hand of shortness."

"What happened to them?"

"They were executed," Hardwic said, his voice no more than a whisper.

"I'm so sorry." Makellos felt a lump form in his throat.

Hardwic glanced up at Makellos. "Thank you. They still live in my heart."

"I don't understand how you can seem so cheerful after suffering such a loss," Makellos said.

Hardwic hummed as he looked up and out the window into the darkness beyond. "As tough as it is, life goes on. I am alive, and I keep their memory alive in me. I know they would not want me to only be sad. I was always quite the cheerful person. The Queen has taken so much from me, but I refuse to let her take that."

"I admire your strength," Makellos said, his eyes turned to the little man with a heart too big for his small frame. "I will do my best to not let her take that from me either."

"I'm certain it is not easy, having her blood in your veins and your closeness to her all of your life. But you seem to be quite a remarkable young man." Hardwic's smile dimpled his cheeks. "I am confident you will rise above the bindings placed upon you."

Six

As the night drew on, there were yawns all around, and a new problem presented itself. In the next room, each of the little men had their own wood-framed bed with a pallet stuffed with straw, rags, and other soft items, and each had a pillow stuffed with feathers that Makellos assumed were probably refreshed from the feathers collected from hunted fowl. But none of the beds were long enough for Makellos to actually stretch out on. Sigurd logically suggested that they could put a few of the beds together to make a larger one.

"Oh no, I couldn't put you out!" Makellos protested.

"That's right," Grimwald said, giving him a cold look. "I ain't giving my bed to some royal."

"Now now, Grim, no need to be rude," said Der, giving him a pointed look over the top of his spectacles.

Makellos wasn't sure why Grimwald didn't like him, but he also was not about to put the hard-working little men out of their own beds. "Please, it's quite all right. I can sleep on the floor."

That set off a round of protests, until Bernhardt reminded everyone of the extra pillows and blankets in the root cellar that were stored for winter. "We could make a comfortable bed on the floor until we can find a better option," he offered.

So, the blankets and pillows were retrieved. The little beds were lined up around the room, but Der suggested they push them all to one side so that the prince could have his own half of the room. Makellos once again protested, but the little men, minus Grimwald, were all in agreement, and the seven little beds were shoved and dragged across the room into a strange jumble of wood frames and blankets.

The room itself was relatively dim. Makellos noted the single window in the room that he had not washed earlier, since he had not entered this room, with bedraggled curtains that could be pulled. There was a chest of drawers that he assumed held clothing, with a pitcher and smaller washbasin upon it, and, by the door, a tarnished-looking full-length mirror on the wall. A door off to the side led to a little washroom, where there also was a battered, discolored copper washbasin, though that was usually for colder weather, Hardwic told him. During the warmer months, they'd make a short trip to the nearby creek and wash there.

With all of the blankets and pillows, which smelled a little musty from the root cellar, Makellos made himself a little nest against the wall opposite the miners. The little men all seemed to have their own processes for getting ready to turn in. A few of them shaved or trimmed their facial hair. Bernhardt sat by one of the windows to smoke a pipe, blowing smoke rings out into the darkness. Makellos took off his waistcoat and boots but left his shirtsleeves and breeches on, both for modesty and for warmth, since he was unsure how cold the night might get.

The little men all settled into their beds; the lantern by the door was blown out, and the room became quite dark except for the dusty blue moonlight filtering in through the window. Makellos pulled one of the blankets over him. His little nook was surprisingly comfortable, certainly preferable to the forest floor, at any rate. But despite his exhaustion, he found he could not sleep right away. He stayed awake, listening to the sounds of the men falling asleep across from him. Someone had an exceptionally loud snore, he couldn't tell who, but he saw someone else sit up and whap them with a pillow, which quieted the noise for a time.

At most, he had only ever had guards or a faithful servant in his room at night. Even out in the woods, his only bedfellows had been the family of squirrels. But now, he was in a strange, new place, with strange, new people. People who had (mostly) agreed to protect him and let him stay as a member of their family, while hardly knowing anything but his name. They had been acquainted for a mere few hours, but he already felt much more comfortable here than he ever had at the palace, where his mother criticized and the servants whispered. He was only going to stay for a few months, but he was absolutely grateful for that time. He would work hard and do his best to earn his keep here, and prove to Grimwald that he was not just a spoiled little prince. He would prove that he was different than the cruel woman who had birthed him.

He must have slept hard once he actually fell asleep, for when he woke up the next morning, sunlight was peeking into the room through the grimy window, and several of the little men were already up and about. There seemed to be quite the kerfuffle happening in regards to finding clothing and using the washbasin, the mirror, the water closet, and pretty much every other space that was available. Makellos decided to stay out of the way of those preparing for work. Instead, he slid on his boots and his waistcoat. His breeches and shirtsleeves were no worse off than the night before, the dust from the blankets disappearing from them as soon as he stood up. A fight broke out between Sigmund and Sigurd over the ownership of a wooden comb as Makellos headed into the main room.

Dagobert was already out there, stoking the embers of the fire. Makellos gave him a smile. "Good morning. Did you sleep well?"

Dagobert looked up in surprise, then beamed and nodded, pointing to Makellos. "Yes, I slept surprisingly well, thank you. May I help you with breakfast?"

Dagobert nodded again and pointed to a nearby loaf of bread, making a slicing motion with his hands. Makellos set about slicing the bread and then toasting it over the fire. The little house was filled with chatter and movement as the men all got ready for the day. They all sat down to a quick breakfast of toast with fruit preserves and a tea made from some sort of root that Makellos didn't know. When Makellos offered to pack some additional food for them, Hardwic explained that they each received a single meal at the mines, usually bread and cheese and a few vegetables, courtesy of an arrangement with the Thieves Guild. That surprised Makellos, both that the little men were given a meal at all, and that the Thieves Guild, of whom he was aware but not very familiar, would have created such an arrangement. He had always thought it to be a gallery of rogues and cutpurses, but it seemed that he had been wrong about that too. There was so much he was learning about the kingdom that he was supposed to be supporting, so much that had been hidden from him.

"We better be off," said Grimwald, shoving a last bite of toast into his mouth with a slight glower at Makellos.

"Indeed. Take care of the prince today, doc," Hardwic said with a cheery smile as the little men all stood and made their way toward the door. Der remained where he was, his cheeks apple-red as the rest departed, carrying tools and bags over their shoulders as they vanished into the woods.

"Doc?" Makellos asked curiously as he set about gathering the dishes from the table.

"My nickname is doc," said Der with a slightly sheepish grin as he rose to his own feet.

"Are you a doctor?" Makellos asked in surprise.

"I was an apothecary, many years ago," Der said. "I learned a lot about medicine and illnesses from treating them, though I've had no formal medical training."

"I suppose that comes in quite handy though, with all of you out here," Makellos said thoughtfully.

"Oh, yes, quite often," Der said, giving a proud little nod.

"How do you get supplies?" Makellos asked, looking around. "The things you can't hunt?"

"Well, you see, we are not allowed in the town surrounding the palace, by the Queen's orders, but we are allowed within the forest. And there are several markets that happen, usually weekly or monthly. We are not given any pay for working in the mines, so we usually trade for the things we need. I make various herbal remedies that I sell or trade. Sigurd and Sigmund are quite the woodworkers, so they make most anything we need from wood, and a few things to sell as well."

Makellos frowned. "I am so sorry for what you have all gone through. It's not fair to you, or to your families."

Der placed a hand lightly on Makellos' arm. "Thank you, your highness. We know you are not to blame, of course."

Makellos gave him a small smile. "The others seem to look to you. Are you the leader, then?"

Der blushed, ducking his head a bit. "Oh, well, I wouldn't say the leader. We try to live in harmony without leaders. But I do feel that sometimes I am the one looked to in a pinch."

"I noticed that," Makellos said with a smile, remembering their arrival yesterday when everyone was behind Der and telling him to talk to Makellos on their behalf. "And I thank you again for your kindness."

Der fumbled one of the dishes in his hands, and Makellos quickly reached down to help steady them, catching Der's hands in between his own. The man's face went bright pink, and he cleared his throat. "Thank you. I am sorry that you are having to escape from such horribleness yourself, your highness."

"Please. Makellos," the prince reminded him with a sweet smile. "I am no more royalty here than anyone else."

Der still looked flustered as he set about cleaning up, and Makellos left him to his tasks. He would do his own scrubbing today; the rest of the windows, more laundry, perhaps the floors and even the walls. He wondered as he worked if Hans had returned yet to the palace to face the Queen and what he would tell her. Perhaps he would lie and say he completed the task, but Makellos had a terrible feeling that his mother would know if the huntsman lied. He hated to think what would happen to Hans. He harbored no illusions that the Queen would just dismiss the insubordination. Hans had been loyal to the Queen for as long as Makellos had known him, but whether that loyalty was actual fealty or fear, he had never known. Now, he suspected the latter.

Seven

Hans returned to the palace at the end of the appointed week he was given to complete his gruesome task. He had spent the last few days of his journey trying to decide what to do. The Queen expected him to return with proof he had slaughtered the prince. He supposed it was possible that Makellos was dead in the woods somewhere. He had fled with nothing but the clothes on his back, and Hans suspected that the forest would not be kind to the pampered young man. But if he tracked him down again, and Makellos was still alive, what then? He would be back in the exact same predicament he had faced before. And he might not have the courage to spare the prince a second time. No, he had to live with the decision he made. But now he had to bear the weight of the choice to let Makellos flee.

The morning after he let the prince go, he found a boar near a river. He felled it with one shot and then proceeded to butcher it. Better the blood of a pig on his hands than the blood of a boy. He removed its liver and lungs, trying not to imagine what it would have been like to see the young prince he had known all of his life splayed out on the grass at his feet. He didn't think he could have borne the sorrow and shame.

Placing the boar's lungs and liver into the jeweled box that glittered obscenely in the blood-streaked grass, he snapped it shut and put it into his bag. If he was lucky, Makellos was no longer alive, through no direct violence from Hans' hand, and the Queen need never know the difference. But, he suspected, he would not be that fortunate. And, he realized, letting the prince starve or be torn apart by wild beasts was much less merciful than a quick and clean death would have been at his hands. What was the point of letting the boy go if he had only condemned him to more suffering? Well, it was done now. So, Hans returned to the palace as late on the final day of the week as he could.

The Queen had been distracted the last few days, he heard as he entered the gates. Something about a boy and spinning something into gold and some other gossip that he was too distracted to pay attention to. But as soon as she heard that Hans had arrived back, the Queen summoned him, not to her throne room, but to her private chamber. He waited outside the door of the elegant rooms, his own travel-worn garb feeling even more out of place in the privacy of her luxurious quarters.

"Ah, my faithful huntsman has returned," the Queen said from where she sat at her desk. "I take it you have completed your mission?" Her ruby lips curved into a cold smirk, for she knew he would not have dared to return otherwise.

"Yes, my Queen," he said, bowing his head from the doorway.

Queen Schön held up her hand, gesturing to the desk in front of her. "And you have brought me the proof I asked for?"

"Yes, my Queen," he said again, moving into the room with the trepidation of entering a tiger's lair or a viper's den. He reached into his bag and produced the jeweled box. The Queen tapped one of her long fingernails on the desk, and he set down the box in front of her with another bow.

The Queen reached over and flipped up the lid of the box to see the viscera within while Hans' heart pounded like a war drum in his chest. A wicked smile spread over the Queen's lips. "Excellent work, my loyal huntsman. You have served me well."

Hans nodded. "Thank you, your majesty," he mumbled. She had not immediately noticed any issues, which was one hurdle passed.

"Tell me, where is the rest of his body?"

"I left him where I felled him, your majesty, deep within the woods." The lie felt as sour as bile on his tongue, and his voice trembled just the faintest bit. But the Queen must have believed it to be reticence at the distasteful act, for she simply waved her hand in dismissal. He bowed again, then turned and left her chambers. And kept walking.

Without a moment's hesitation, he walked through the palace, to the stables, grabbed the fastest horse they had, not even bothering to put a saddle upon it, and rode it out of the gates, stealing away like a thief in the night. Better to be alive and on the run than condemned and chained in darkness or whatever torture the Queen might decide for him. He had been loyal to the crown his whole life, and the crown no longer deserved him.

With preparations being made in the throne room for the final test of the boy, whatever his name was, to spin straw into gold, the Queen did not go immediately to her magic mirror. She had not given thought to her child one day outshining her, and she would not take that risk again now that the threat had been eliminated.

When she finally stepped into her workshop off of her chambers, she approached the mirror with the jeweled box in her hands. "Magic mirror on the wall, who is the fairest of them all?"

"Famed is thy beauty, Majesty," the mirror said. "But there is yet one fairer still."

"Who is it?" she demanded, her jaw clenching, her lips setting into a firm line. Was there already a new threat to her?

"He is known to thee by three names, Majesty," the mirror intoned. "Prince. Son."

"Stop!" the Queen commanded, holding up her hand. She opened the box and held it up. "Makellos is dead. The huntsman has brought me proof."

"Prince Makellos still lives," the mirror said with its usual detached tone, for what did magic care for emotion? "While he still breathes, his fairness outshines yours. 'Tis the innards of a boar in your bejeweled chest."

For just a moment, Queen Schön stood, stunned and speechless as the words echoed inside her mind. And then a scream tore from her throat, and she threw the box hard against the wall. It shattered into pieces, and the organs within splattered into a lumpy, bloody mess on the stone floor. She seethed with rage, for she had been tricked, disobeyed, played for a fool by one of her most loyal servants. She realized she had chosen a man. A weak-hearted fool, too influenced by tears and feelings. She should have used her more powerful weapon to begin with. She schooled her features once more into calm elegance. "Mirror, mirror. Show me my Shadow."

She waited as her dark magic seeped through the mirror to summon the geist to her. And she waited. And waited another moment longer. He had never before ignored her summons. Of all of the times he could have tested her patience, this was not the one to choose. Flaming hot fury rose in her again, this time prompted by her Shadow's resistance. "Mirror, mirror. Show me my Shadow!"

Dark swirls began to coalesce, and then the image of her geist appeared, wearing only boots and his breeches. Her temper flared further. Some nasty little slattern had been distracting her Shadow from his singular duty. "Where have you been, Pet?" she cooed, her tone high and syrupy sweet. "Did I interrupt your business in one of my whorehouses?"

The look in the creature's dark eyes when he looked up into hers was not unfamiliar, but even though she knew he loathed her with all of his non-existent heart, she had come to the end of her tolerance for his insolence. She narrowed her eyes, which was all the warning she gave him before she sent a powerful blast of magic into the center of his body where her enchantment resided. He crumpled to his knees, where he belonged.

"No one," she hissed. "No one is more important than me." Her Shadow had been acting strangely the past few days. But she was the only master he would serve. She would find whoever was distracting her assassin and crush them like a flea pulled from a dog.

The furious release of magic had gone through her like an arrow through an apple, and she smoothed her hands over her bodice as she let out another angry breath. She took a deeper one now, lifting her chin to gaze down her nose once more at the creature. "When I summon you, Pet, you come. Have I made myself clear?"

He didn't respond. He didn't have to. She could see his resolve in his eyes.

"I learned some very... disturbing news before I retired to bed. A reliable source informed me that a problem I thought had been resolved is, in fact, not." His head stayed bowed in silence. "You are to locate someone for me." He still did not move. He was either being defiant or submissive, and she honestly didn't care which. As long as he did his duty, he could sulk all he liked. "My son is alive... I need him found."

Eight

Though he was only spending his third night in the little cottage, Makellos found that he was increasingly comfortable here. The little men were very appreciative of his willingness to help in whatever way he could, and other than having to hunt for meat, the little homestead was very self-sufficient. There was still a lot of work to be done every day, and he was unsurprised that they had not been able to keep up with it when they were already working so hard in the mines. He too was exhausted from all the work around the house, but he would not complain. He was eternally grateful to them for the roof over his head and the food in his stomach.

Today, Hardwic had been the one to stay home, and he had spent most of the day away hunting, so Makellos had worked alone, continuing with his scrubbing of the cottage. They planned that Makellos would learn to chop wood the next day with Grim, and he would fix the roof later this week with Sigurd. There were still a lot of preparations that needed to be done before snow fell, and he was happy to help however he could.

He slid off his white shirtsleeves as he prepared for bed, hanging them on a hook nearby to smooth it out, still its same pristine white as always. At least it was one set of clothing he didn't have to worry about washing, which left him time for others. He yawned, stretching his neck and shoulders, and then leaned down to pull back the blanket from his comfortable nest.

The back of his neck prickled. Someone was watching him. He straightened up and turned quickly toward the full-length mirror by the doorway. But of course, no one was watching him from the mirror. Instead, Sigmund stood framed in the door, leaning casually on one arm as he gave the prince a once-over look and an appreciative wolf-whistle. Makellos very nearly covered himself like a virginal milkmaid, but he forced his arms to stay where they were. He wasn't in the palace anymore, he reminded himself. Here, he was not a prince. He had to earn his keep, and if letting the little men ogle him once in a while was the price he had to pay, well, he supposed it was a reasonable currency. And Sigmund was certainly not terrible to look at. None of the little men were, if he was being honest.

"See something you like, I take it," he said, giving Sigmund a small smile. Was that how one flirted? Was that what he was trying to do? Flirt? He had not had much opportunity to do so elsewhere. Most of his interactions with others were strictly formal, and, because of his station, people would laugh and respond positively even if he said something entirely foolish, so it was quite hard to know if he was doing well at anything at all.

"I certainly do," Sigmund said with another grin.

"Keep it in your breeches," muttered Grimwald, shoving past Sigmund. Sigmund rolled his eyes but gave Makellos a wink.

"Some other time."

"I'll be here," Makellos said, and then spent the next two hours unable to fall asleep as he contemplated how ridiculous of an answer that had been.

Something moved over him, something that made every hair on his body stand up, though he didn't know why. He was choking. He was drowning. There was no air. Somewhere inside of his mind, Makellos realized that the distress he was feeling wasn't only a dream. His eyes flew open to a darkness that was so deep, it seemed to engulf him in a sea of nothingness.

Gazing down at him was the Queen's Shadow. The geist she had enslaved so many years ago, the specter that he had grown up being afraid of and spent most of his time avoiding in the palace. In the suffocating darkness, his eyes and cheeks looked even more ghastly in his pale, angular face. Makellos' hands flew up to his throat where the geist's shadows wrapped around him, his heart racing frantically in his chest. He tried to claw at the tightness that gripped him, but he might as well have tried to hold on to smoke. He couldn't even scream to alert the miners to the unnatural presence in the room.

The Shadow had to be here to kill him because the Queen had discovered that Hans had let Makellos go. When her first attempt had failed, she had sent her most powerful assassin to ensure the job was completed. His lungs burned, the pressure in his body so tremendous, he wondered if his skin might split. He was going to die here, for nothing more than his mother's vanity.

Makellos' vision flickered, and, for a moment, he thought the world had gone strangely purple. It was then that he realized there was a glow emanating from the tendrils that encircled his throat, a strange violet light that licked over them like flames and then up toward the outstretched hand of the Shadow. The geist took a large step back, the shadows falling away from him, the pressure on his neck suddenly gone. Makellos sucked in a breath of the sweetest air he had ever breathed before the coughing started; choked, painful sounds halfway between a gasp and a sob. He realized a moment later that someone else besides him was desperately drawing in air. The Queen's Shadow doubled over and dropped to the floor. The cocoon of darkness he had woven around them was falling and disintegrating, like water poured over a wall of spun sugar, and the unnatural silence now became punctuated with the sounds of seven other individuals in a room in various stages of sleep.

Unable to do more than take in gulping mouthfuls of air, Makellos coughed again, flailing against the blankets that had twisted around him, fighting them as if they too were trying to bring him harm. His ears were ringing, tears beginning to run down his cheeks as he choked on each desperate breath.

He wasn't sure which of the little men awoke first, but there was suddenly shouting, and then the room erupted in a cacophony of chaos. The miners were scrambling out of bed, crashing into one another in the dim light and the tight quarters. He blinked several times to try to clear his vision, just in time to see the Shadow haul himself to the tall, discolored looking glass by the door and begin to disappear into it.

One of the miners, he couldn't tell who, was by his side, a hand on his back in kind reassurance. He could hear vague shouts of, "Get him!" and "The mirror!" from the miners. There was another mad scramble as some of the men tried to chase the Shadow while others tried to get to Makellos.

The Queen's Shadow finally vanished through the mirror, and with him, the remaining vestiges of the unnatural darkness he had ensconced the room in. The last of his head and shoulders had just disappeared into the tarnished surface of the looking-glass when, with a growl, Grimwald grabbed the nearest heavy object, which happened to be the pitcher off the washstand, and threw it against the mirror with all of his might. The pitcher and the mirror exploded and shattered into several large pieces and hundreds of tiny shards, tinkling to the wooden floor of the cottage.

And then there was a stunned silence, punctuated only by Makellos' ragged breathing. Someone lit the lantern by the door and carried it closer to him. The light stung his eyes, making tears well again, and the light moved to not be so close to his face.

"Der," one of the men said. "You better check him out."

"Oh, uh, yes, yes," Der said, turning back to the pile of beds to find his spectacles that had been lost in the pandemonium.

It hurt to swallow. It even hurt to breathe. Makellos coughed again, and several hands rubbed his back and shoulders comfortingly. His eyes were still hot and full of tears. He didn't want to cry, but there seemed to be no way to clear them other than to let them fall, so he did.

"There, there," cooed a warm voice by his left shoulder. Hardwic, he thought. "We've got you. Just breathe."

"Someone fetch him some water," said Sigurd on his right.

Der finally emerged from the mess with his spectacles on, his hair sticking up in every direction, making his way over to Makellos. "Let me have a look. Dagobert, hold that lamp up high so I can see."

Sigurd held one hand while Sigmund held the other. Makellos' hands trembled in theirs as Der's warm, calloused fingers prodded and stroked over his throat. He opened his mouth when instructed, and Der tipped his head this way and that, trying to look down his throat. "How's it look, doc?" Sigurd asked.

"Well, a little bruising, but nothing seems broken," Der said with a reassuring smile. "A few days of rest, and no talking, and you should be good as new."

"But-" Makellos started, horrified by the rasp that came from his throat.

Der held up a stern finger. "No talking unless it's an emergency."

Makellos nodded, then glanced down as Bernhardt appeared in front of him, holding a mug of cool water. He took it with a grateful smile and tried to swallow a mouthful. It hurt, and he sputtered a cough. Sigurd and Sigmund both patted his back to help him clear it, and he took another careful sip.

"Well, it's obvious the Queen knows he's alive and is looking for him," Sigmund said with a dramatic sigh.

"With the mirror destroyed, she shouldn't be able to see you, right?" Bernhardt asked Makellos.

Makellos shook his head.

"Can she transport herself?" Hardwic asked worriedly. "Could she be on her way to us right now?"

Makellos shook his head again. In his twenty winters, he had never seen his mother teleport or transport herself some place, no matter how much of a rush she was in.

"What do you suppose pulled away the Queen's Shadow?" asked Bernhardt thoughtfully.

Makellos shook his head yet again. He had spent most of his childhood avoiding the geist whenever possible. His gory work and cruel stare made Makellos' blood run cold in his veins. But he had never imagined his mother would send her Shadow after him, of all people. Something had to have gone wrong back at the palace or with the shadow creature, for Makellos had never known him to not complete a task he had been given. His lethality was legendary.

"Well, it's pretty much morning," Hardwic said, glancing out the grimy window. "It's your turn to stay home, isn't it, Grim?"

Grimwald nodded slowly, his eyebrows knitting together. "I'll keep an eye out for the old witch today, just in case."

"And at night, we should find a way to protect the prince, since the Queen knows he's alive," Sigurd said thoughtfully.

"Well, we can stew on it and figure it out tonight," Der said. He glanced out the window where the sky was more of a charcoal than an inky black. "We should get going anyway."

Nine

After final reassurances that Makellos felt all right and that he would keep his talking to a minimum, six of the little men set out for the mines as the sun painted the sky with broad strokes of the most incredible colors. It was quite beautiful, Makellos mused to himself as he watched them go. Grimwald stayed behind today. He started to gather the dirty dishes, but Makellos shook his head, taking them from Grim's hands. He patted his chest, letting Grim know that he could take care of it.

Grim gazed back at him before he sighed thickly and nodded. "All right. 'Smy job to cut wood anyway, and we need a hell of a lot of it come winter. So, I'll be out front if you need me."

Makellos nodded eagerly again, and Grim headed out the door. Makellos cleaned up the dishes and breakfast. He watched out the front window as he did. He thought that Grim must have been a woodcutter earlier in his life, for he swung the ax with practiced ease, splitting each log with precision. Makellos made his way out to the garden to pick some vegetables to prepare for the evening's dinner. He was in the garden, only a short distance away, when the steady sound of Grim's work stopped. He glanced up to see the man peel off his sweat-soaked shirt and toss it aside. Despite his small stature, the years of work in the mines and chopping wood had given the man an amazingly sculpted torso and arms. Makellos found himself staring. He was not usually one to gawk at anyone; his mother would scold him for his rudeness. And, she reminded him, a prince was above all others. He was to be stared at, not to do the staring himself.

Grim picked up the ax and swung it up over his head, bringing it down with a vicious whack that split the wood into two pieces. Makellos nearly dropped the basket of vegetables he held as he watched the little man's muscles twist and flex in the sunlight, dotted all over with little beads of shining perspiration. His face went red, though it had nothing to do with his aching throat. He headed back inside the cottage as quickly as he could, having to take a few deep breaths to calm his racing heart and rushing blood.

He had never had that reaction to anyone before. Not that he had many opportunities to see partially-naked men or women in the palace anyway. Many of the servants were so afraid of the Queen that none of them had ever tried to seduce him that he was aware of. He didn't blame them, for nothing good could come of a servant, or even a noble, openly courting him in front of his mother.

Once he had himself back under control, Makellos made a drink of a few crushed fruits before going back out to where Grim worked, holding out the mug in offering. Grimwald set the ax down, looking surprised but held out his hands for it. Makellos gave it to him, and Grim swallowed several mouthfuls. "Damn. That's pretty good," he said, peering into the mug. "Thanks."

Makellos nodded, then glanced down at the ax. He had never chopped wood before either, and he was sure Grim could use a little break. He pointed to the ax, then held out his hands, offering to give it a try himself. Grim glowered at him. "You're not doing that, *Snow White.*" He said the name like it hurt his mouth to form the words.

Makellos frowned and reached for the ax, but Grim grabbed it and pulled it back. "It's hard work. Too hard for your soft hands."

Makellos glared, putting said soft hands on his hips. Just because he was not used to the work did not mean that he could not or did not want to help out. Everyone had to start doing things without experience, after all.

Grim gazed back at him for a moment before his shoulders loosened, and he sighed. "Look, I'll teach ya how to cut wood. But not right now. You're injured. Once you're recovered." Makellos lifted a dark, skeptical brow. "I promise," Grim said with a huff.

Makellos held out his hand to the man to shake. Grim stared at it in surprise, looking up into Makellos' blue eyes. After a moment, he lifted his own hand and hocked an impressive wad of spit into it, offering it out to the prince.

Makellos recoiled for a moment, staring. That was disgusting. Grim gave him a small smirk and dropped the hand again. Makellos' eyes narrowed. He would not let Grim get the better of him or continue to think of him as some sort of spoiled brat who could not hold his own. He had said he was going to be part of this group, and he would be. He lifted his own hand to his mouth, summoning as much saliva as he could on a whim, and spat it into his own hand. Much less impressive than Grim's, but he didn't care, just holding out his hand to seal the agreement.

Grim stared at him for a long moment before the corner of his lip twitched upward in an appreciative smile, and he slapped his hand into Makellos', giving it a shake. "Guess you better recover fast, kid." Makellos blew him a playful kiss, and Grim actually laughed, the sound loud and boisterous. "All right, all right, get back to your own work." Makellos turned to head back into the cottage, but he did not miss seeing the bright red spots that bloomed on Grimwald's cheeks when he blew him that kiss.

Even though he was still working hard, Makellos noticed that Grimwald did several laps around the area of the cottage under the guise of grabbing more wood. But Makellos could see him holding his ax defensively, his eyes darting back and forth through the trees. When a large buck ventured close to the house, Grim yelled and raced at it, and the buck darted away. Makellos smiled to himself. Grim really was serious about making sure that he was safe should the Queen attempt another attack. It worried him that she knew that Hans had lied and that he still lived. He wondered if the merciful huntsman, usually so loyal to his mother, was still alive and what might have become of him. He also could only hope that the Shadow had not told her where to find him. He didn't know the extent of the geist's powers, or even exactly how his mother controlled him. He could also only hope that if there was another attempt made on his life, the little men who had been so kind to him would not be harmed.

Once the others had returned and eaten the hearty stew Makellos had prepared, the topic was broached again of sleeping arrangements.

"Should we sleep in shifts?" suggested Sigurd.

Makellos frowned and shook his head at that. The little men already worked so hard every day, they all needed as much rest as they could get. He did not want to add an extra burden onto them over an attempt that might not even happen.

Sigmund gave a mischievous, little smile. "Put all the beds together and sleep around the prince?"

Makellos felt his face go red for the second time that day. He ducked his head a little, peering up at the little men with a slightly shy smile. He had never shared a bed before with anyone, though he realized that he did not oppose the idea. If the Shadow, or anyone else, attacked him again when they were all gathered together, someone would wake up sooner.

"Would that be all right, your highness?" Bernhardt asked. "We just want to keep you safe, should the Queen make another attempt."

Makellos smiled again. "You all are very sweet. But you don't need to put yourself in danger for my sake." His voice still had a rasp to it, but he could tell it was already getting better from his day of imposed silence.

"Oh, shut up, that wasn't the question," Grim grumbled.

Makellos felt his whole body burn. He had never in his life been told to 'shut up,' but the way Grimwald had said it held a note of affection that made his insides flutter in a strange way.

"You are one of us," Bernhardt said, giving him a reassuring smile. "We will not let you be hurt again."

Makellos swallowed and glanced around at the seven little miners. "As long as I do not put anyone out of their beds," he said.

Dagobert gave a little whoop of delight, which set off laughter all around.

So, the seven little bedframes were pushed together so that all eight of them could stretch out upon them, with the nest of blankets from Makellos' previous bed being added for additional support and comfort. Makellos wasn't sure whether he would be able to easily fall asleep. He had never shared a bed with anyone before, let alone with seven others. And, he realized now, each of the little men had their own level of comfort for night attire, from Der in a full nightgown and cap, to Bernhardt, who was dressed in nothing at all until he realized that Makellos was watching him with embarrassment, and he drew on a loose pair of breeches that were decidedly not his from the way they hung on his tiny body.

Makellos kept his white shirtsleeves and breeches on tonight as he slid under the covers in the center of the makeshift bed. Once he had settled and had a blanket over him, the seven little men all slid into the bed as well. There was much squirming and a few curses as they all tried to find a comfortable spot, but finally they all seemed settled in, gathered around Makellos from his head to his feet. The warmth and heaviness from the bodies around him was oddly comforting as Makellos closed his eyes. He was a little worried that fear of the geist coming back would keep him awake, but within only a few minutes, he had drifted off into a comfortable and relaxed sleep.

Ten

Makellos woke up feeling warmer than he ever had in his life. It took him a moment to realize where he was and why things seemed different. His blue eyes peeked open to find the thatched eves and ceiling of the cottage above him. There was weight on him in several places. His eyes traveled downward then, and his brain finally understood why he was so warm. He had a thick hide blanket over him, and he was surrounded on all sides by the seven little miners. Each of them was asleep, curled up on either side of him, like a cozy pile of sleeping puppies. He could feel an arm draped over his side to splay on his chest, the palm and fingers small but very warm.

And then he realized, with a shameful realization, that he was hard. He hadn't woken up like that since the day he left the palace. His mind had been so afraid and focused on the immediate changes. But now, here, in a comfortable bed, with a good night's sleep, and seven admittedly very attractive men cuddled against him, evidently his mind had decided that his cock's hiatus was over. He flushed. Perhaps he could get it to go away before everyone woke, or perhaps he could extricate himself from the pile and take himself to the washroom until he had calmed. He started to squirm, but the arm holding him only gripped tighter, and he felt someone else by his knees stir, and he went still again. So much for that second plan. Hopefully he could lie here motionless enough without waking anyone that his morning wood would go down on its own.

And then he realized that someone was watching him. It took him a moment to realize who. It was Sigmund, who was lying on his side at about the level of his ribcage. The man's hazel eyes were on his face, and Makellos felt a blush color his cheeks. Sigmund shifted, and Makellos was mortified to feel the man's body press against his in such a way that there would be no doubt of his current predicament, rubbing up against the man's torso through the fabric of his breeches. Sigmund kept eye contact with Makellos as his hand slid, slowly and carefully, under the blanket, watching for any sign that Makellos wanted him to stop. Makellos' breath caught in his chest, his heart fluttering faster. The hand rested questioningly on the prince's stomach, and, ever so slowly, Makellos gave him a little nod.

Sigmund gave him a playful, knowing smile before Makellos felt the man's hand slide down his lower stomach to give him a squeeze between his legs. Makellos clamped his lips together over the sudden noise that tried to escape his throat, managing to turn it into an exhalation through his nose, but his eyes went wide. Sigmund grinned broader, his hand suddenly sliding against skin as it dipped under the waist of the breeches and began moving down the soft expanse of skin between naval and desire. His fingers, rough and calloused but also incredibly warm, brushed through the dark hair at the base of Makellos' cock, and then over said cock itself. Makellos inhaled again. Sigmund's eyes flickered with a question, unspoken but for a slight tip of his head.

Makellos found himself struck by rather a conundrum. Sigmund had been flirting with him for days, and Makellos was delighted to find that he felt similar feelings. But, he realized, they were also in a bed with six other individuals. He knew that these men had shared this little cottage for years, so inevitably someone must have had some sort of awkward encounter at some time. But the impropriety of it, especially with them still being relative strangers to one another, and his own lack of experience made this whole moment seem rather unfortunate timing. His eyes flicked around to the sleepers around them, then back to Sigmund. Sigmund shrugged and gave Makellos a smile back that could only be interpreted as wicked. He watched as the man's chestnut head suddenly dipped under the heavy blanket, and then he could feel the man's fingers working deftly at the fastenings of his breeches. His breath quickened with each movement, until Sigmund's fingers undid them fully, then reached in and slid his cock out of the fabric that had been restraining it. He instantly felt the coolness and the relief of not being trapped in the tight fabric anymore, then clapped his own hand to his mouth to smother the sound that came out of him as he felt hot, wet lips wrap around the head of his cock and a warm tongue brush up the underside. It felt like every hair on his body suddenly stood at attention as Sigmund's mouth wrapped around the tip and sucked lightly, swirling his tongue around. Makellos squeaked softly through his nose, then quickly pinched that closed too with his thumb and forefinger. Sigmund's lips wrapped around him again as he sucked, his head bobbing a little as he slid further down Makellos' shaft.

Makellos realized he had cut off his own breathing, and he released his nose with a soft gasping sound as he saw stars in front of his eyes, both from the lack of oxygen, and from the warm, tight heat sliding further down his cock in a delicious sensation he had never experienced before. And then Sigmund buried his nose in Makellos' thicket of dark curls, his breath warm, his tongue tracing up the underside in a way that made the prince's head spin. He moaned, the sound muffled by his hand, and he quickly tried to stifle it further, but then Sigmund began to bob his head, and Makellos exhaled sharply again with a soft whimper.

Someone else stirred, and Makellos went rigid and still. But he was unsuccessful in stopping another moan that escaped him as Sigmund's tongue teased up and down, and Hardwic's green eyes opened and turned toward him. Makellos felt himself flush all over, trying to hold still like he was perfectly innocent, but he could see Sigmund moving up and down his cock under the blanket, leaving no question as to what he was doing.

Hardwic let out a bark of laughter that startled awake Der and Bernhardt, and the others around them stirred as well. Makellos felt his mortification grow as Sigmund continued his ministrations, heedless of the fact that there were suddenly six other people now awake in the bed, their eyes darting between Makellos' face and the bobbing of the blanket at crotch level.

"Well, well," said Sigurd, next to his brother. He reached down and suddenly flipped back the hide blanket, and Makellos thought he might actually die of embarrassment. Sigmund continued to fellate him eagerly, raising his eyes to meet Bernhardt's, who was directly across from him, giving him a rather smug look.

They were all awake now, so Makellos removed his hand from his mouth, scrambling for the blanket again. "I'm sorry!" he said, pushing Sigmund up and off of his cock with a sudden obscene pop that had his cheeks flaming as red as apples. "Please forgive- I... shouldn't have- didn't... mean to..." He stumbled out of the bed, dragging the hide blanket with him, knocking Dagobert and Bernhardt onto the floor where they had been lying on it. He stumbled toward the water closet, tripping over his breeches and blanket but trying to keep some shred of modesty as he hobbled like a wounded fowl toward it. He still babbled mindless apologies until he stumbled into the water closet and shut the door firmly.

He sank to the floor, feeling hot and shameful all over. He had never given in to lust like that before, and in front of the little men who had all been so kind to him! He quickly wiggled his breeches back on, trying to tuck himself away as best he could while still painfully hard, his balls heavy and aching for release. But no, they had all watched him come in here, and the thought of giving himself relief while they all stared at the closed doorway was too much.

But now he had to go and face them. Or he could just hide in this water closet until all but one of them left for work, which didn't seem very practical, since they would need to come in here themselves to prepare for the day. His heart was racing. Would they think him terrible? So depraved that he had to slag his lust like that? Would they send him away?

He could hear quiet mumbles and movement from the other side of the door, but he couldn't make out any particular words. Someone tapped lightly on the door, nearly making him leap out of his skin. "Who is it?" he asked, feeling utterly foolish, curled on the floor in a blanket.

"It's Bernhardt," came the man's thin, wizened voice. "Are you all right, your highness?"

"Yes." The sound came out much too high and fast, and Makellos cringed at his own reaction. "Yes, I... I'm fine. How are you?"

There was a soft chuckle from the other side of the door. "You have nothing to be embarrassed about, lad," Bernhardt said, his voice kind and soothing. "Really, it's all right."

Makellos hesitantly got to his knees, the blanket wrapped over his head like a nun's habit, clutched to his throat, as he opened the door slowly. Sitting on his knees, he was nearly the same height at little Bernhardt. The older man's eyes, the gray of a stormy afternoon, gazed back at him. "I'm so terribly sorry," he said, glancing past Bernhardt to see that the little men were all out of bed now and were either pulling on clothing or had moved out to the main room. "I shouldn't have done that."

"Why not?" Bernhardt asked.

"It... it was dreadfully wicked of me," Makellos said, though he could hear the uncertainty in his own tone.

"Did you want him to do that?" Bernhardt asked, tipping his head slightly.

Makellos' cheeks flushed scarlet again. "Yes," he said softly. "Please do not be upset with Sigmund."

Bernhardt let out another chuckle. "My boy. You have done absolutely nothing wrong, nothing to be forgiven for. If you wanted it, and he wanted to give it, where is the harm in it?"

"It was not an appropriate time or place," Makellos said.

For just a moment, Bernhardt's smile became a bit... Makellos thought almost sad. "We have lived here together longer than you've been alive, dear lad. There is very little that is private between all of us."

"But surely... *that* sort of thing is something you try to keep private?"

Bernhardt laughed, the sound surprisingly kind and sweet. "What do you suppose happens when you put seven men together for years? We've all seen and done things that would make your hair stand up. And not only your hair, but your eyebrows and your cock as well."

Makellos' face went scarlet, and he ducked his head down. "You're not bashful at all, are you?"

"Not a bit," Bernhardt said with a rather boyish grin on his elderly face. "People already discount me so much, if I did not speak up for myself, I would never be noticed at all. And if I am not confident, I am not taken seriously. Now, will you please come out of the wash room, and we can talk further?"

Makellos pushed himself to his feet, his cock now thankfully flaccid in his breeches. He stepped out, and Grim shoved past him, slamming the door to the water closet behind him. Bernhardt reached up and took Makellos' hand, leading him back over to the bed where the whole debacle had started. Makellos sat down uneasily, letting the hide blanket fall down.

Bernhardt smiled, his face gentle and kind. "Listen now. What you felt and what you wanted, there's nothing wrong with it. Perhaps it felt odd to be in such an awkward place as with others in the bed around you, but we have seen it all, I promise you. It was not incredibly long ago that we even committed such acts together."

"We? You mean, all of you?" Makellos asked in surprise.

Bernhardt nodded, rubbing a tiny hand over his bushy beard. "We each have our own relationships and desires, but it's been so long since we've acted on most of them. There's just too much work to be done, and one's body and spirit can only do so much."

"I understand that," Makellos said, realizing that in the hierarchy of priorities, sexual needs were likely nowhere near the top. "I am not used to... I haven't..."

Bernhardt smiled sagely. "No explanation is necessary. Please. Do not shame yourself or hold yourself to blame for trying to find a bit of happiness in a dark, cruel world."

Makellos felt an unexpected tug inside of him at that. Was that what he had been doing? It made sense. He liked Sigmund. He liked all of the little miners, in their own ways. "I suppose I greatly embarrassed Sigmund. I should apologize."

"No need," said the man himself, coming in from the main room, shirtless and chewing on a piece of bread. "I'm not embarrassed at all. Though I am terribly sorry that you were." He dropped to one knee, bowing his head and taking Makellos' hand. "Please forgive me, your highness," he said, dropping a playful kiss on the back of it.

"No!" Makellos said quickly. "I mean, yes, I mean..." He cleared his throat. "You have nothing to be forgiven for. I am quite all right and just sorry I caused such a commotion."

"I'm sorry we didn't get to finish what we started," Sigmund said, lifting his head and giving Makellos a playful smirk. "Guess it will have to wait until I get back from work."

Makellos felt his cheeks warm, but he nodded slowly. "I... I think I should like that."

"Good. Because I want to taste that incredible cock again," Sigmund said, getting to his feet and winking at Makellos before sauntering over to the dresser to grab a fresh tunic.

Makellos glanced over at Bernhardt, but the older man looked as non-plussed as if they were speaking of the weather. "Thank you for calming me," he said with a laugh that felt a little uneasy still, but he felt much better now.

Bernhardt nodded. "Of course. Please know, your highness, you are free here to develop any relationships you like, with anyone. As long as all are consenting, there is no judgement amongst us."

"I will keep that in mind," Makellos said. "Thank you."

Eleven

Everyone went off to work shortly thereafter except for Sigurd. They were going to fix the roof today. Once all had departed, he watched Sigurd swallow a tincture in a little glass bottle. "What is that for?"

Sigurd swallowed the single mouthful and corked the bottle up again, setting it on the sideboard to wash. "I'm not sure what's all in it, but I'm allergic to something here. Grim thinks it's the mold from the roof. It makes me sneezy when I'm here all day, when the sun shines on the roof. And I'm allergic to sawdust, which is just excellent luck for a carpenter, eh? So, Der compounded this to help my allergies."

"Well, that won't do," Makellos said, glancing up at the patchy roof. "Hopefully taking out the moldy pieces today will help with that."

"I hope so," said Sigurd with a chuckle. "Hey, are you really all right? I know my brother can be a handful sometimes, and he's a dreadful flirt."

"Oh!" Makellos said, laughing a bit. "I'm all right, I promise. I... I just have never... done any of that... before..." His voice grew softer and softer.

"Really?" Sigurd asked as they headed for the nearby creek to collect reeds for the thatch. "A handsome buck like you? You didn't have all of the young men and ladies chasing after you?"

"If they did, they never told me about it," Makellos said with a huffy breath. "But then, my mother was so severe, I didn't really ever consider taking a lover to bed. Any time I became close to a servant or someone in the palace, they would be sent away. My mother didn't want me to have friends 'beneath me.'"

Sigurd clucked his tongue. "And with no siblings, that would be everyone else."

"Yes," Makellos said with a sigh, running his fingers through his dark hair. "It was quite the lonely life sometimes."

"But now you have seven of us," Sigurd said with a gleam in his hazel eyes.

"That I do," Makellos said. "Tell me about you. And your brother. Where are you from?"

"Our family is actually from Hallin," said Sigurd as they reached the creek and began to cut at the reeds. "But Sigmund and I have always lived in Falchovari. Our family were carpenters."

"Der said you made the furniture in the cottage," Makellos said, glad to be able to connect those together. "It's all incredibly beautiful."

"Thank you," Sigurd said, giving Makellos a bright grin reminiscent of Sigmund's. "My brother and I were the only little people in our family. My father never treated us any different than any of his other children. We learned a trade, we got an education, we got married."

"You were married?" Makellos asked in surprise.

"I was," Sigurd said, his eyes on his work so Makellos couldn't see the pain in his face. "I had a wife and a beautiful daughter. They... they actually were in a terrible accident only a year before the Queen rounded us up, and they both passed away. They might have been executed otherwise."

"I'm so sorry," Makellos said softly. "You must miss them terribly."

"Every day," Sigurd said, then cleared his throat as his eyes started to mist. "I might have remarried one day. Sigmund, he wasn't married, but he was engaged. His fiancé was a local farm boy, but of regular height. It was lucky for them they were not married yet, or who knows what might have happened to him."

"Do you know where he is now?" Makellos asked.

Sigurd shook his head. "No. We're not allowed communication from the *outside*." He said it with such loathing that Makellos actually flinched. "I'm sure he's moved on by now. Twenty-two winters is a long time to wait for someone to return."

"What about the others?" Makellos asked.

"Hardwic and Der were both married, but I know their families were all executed," Sigurd said softly. "Bernhardt was always an old bachelor, more concerned with his career. He was an actor, you know. And Dagobert was only six when he was taken from his family. It's a miracle he was sent to the mines instead of executed."

Makellos shuddered. A six-year-old in the mines. The fact that he survived was in itself another miracle. He counted off the little men in his head. "What about Grimwald?"

"Ah, yes." Sigurd said it in such a way that Makellos thought maybe he wouldn't say anything more, but after a long silence, he said, "Grim's lost the most of all of us, I'd say. He had a wife and five little children. All of them small."

"Five children!" Makellos breathed in surprise.

"Yes. Even had a sixth one on the way when it happened. His... his whole family was wiped out, from his wife, down to the littlest babe." Sigurd glanced up at Makellos. "Just... don't tell him I told you, huh? It still hurts like a fresh wound."

Makellos nodded numbly. A wife, five children, another on the way, all gone, and Grimwald had been unable to stop it. The man's prickly demeanor and unwillingness to become close to someone suddenly made a whole lot more sense. "I can't even imagine what he must be going through."

"They were dark days for all of us," Sigurd said, standing straight to stretch out his back. "But especially that."

"I know they are only words, but I am so sorry for what you and the others went through," Makellos said, a tear slipping down his cheek and falling off the end of his nose to plop into the creek.

Sigurd shook his head. "It means a lot. We don't blame you, you know. Shit, you weren't even born when this happened. It was your cunt of a mother, if you'll pardon my language."

Makellos laughed softly. "I have never heard anyone call her that before, but it is definitely applicable."

They made their way home and spent much of the morning and afternoon patching the roof. Sigurd got a face full of straw at one point and sneezed so hard he nearly tipped the ladder backwards. Makellos caught him by the front of his collar and pulled him forward again so he was balanced, but the move brought their faces extremely close together. Sigurd smirked just a bit. "If you haven't done the whole fiddle with anyone, does that mean you've never kissed anyone either?"

Makellos' breath caught in his throat as he looked back into Sigurd's roguish eyes. It was easy to tell that he and Sigmund were brothers, for they had the same mischievous glint. "I... No, I haven't."

"Would you like to?"

"Yes," Makellos said softly, then quickly shook himself out of the momentary reverie. "I would, but perhaps not while on a roof?"

Sigurd laughed brightly. "Fair enough."

They finished the roof just as the sun reached the tops of the trees. They headed back inside, and Sigurd went to wash up while Makellos started on a hearty roast for dinner. He still wanted to wrangle the vegetable garden, but at least it was plentiful, which was helpful considering how many mouths it had to feed.

Sigurd came out of the bedroom, freshly washed, his chestnut hair still damp. He was wearing a pair of breeches but nothing else. Makellos couldn't help but stare a little curiously. Sigurd's torso was relatively large compared to his limbs, but his spine was curved rather sharply, almost seeming to push his torso forward. "May I be terribly rude and ask if that hurts you?" he asked, gesturing to Sigurd's back.

Sigurd chuckled. "Sometimes. But I've lived with it for almost fifty years. It's just the way I am."

Makellos smiled at that. He supposed when one did not have a choice and had known nothing else, being positive was important. "If I may pry a little further... Bernhardt said that some of you developed relationships with one another over the years. Who...

How did...?" Makellos waved a hand, hoping it would articulate what he couldn't find a tactful way to say.

Sigurd at least caught his meaning. "Ah, well. Sometimes it was just desire and willingness. But Der and Hardwic had something going for a long while."

"Oh," said Makellos with a small chuckle. "I could see that."

Sigurd's expression changed to a sly smirk. "Yes. I think *technically* they are still a couple, but with how exhausting things have been recently, they haven't done much together."

"What about you?" Makellos asked curiously. "Anyone in particular that you fancy?"

Sigurd's smirk flickered just a moment, softening into something that looked almost shy, before reverting back to a casual smile that mirrored Sigmund's usual look. "At the moment, just one."

"Oh? Who?" Makellos asked curiously.

Sigurd laughed and rubbed the back of his head with his hand. "I don't think he has really noticed me."

"Who?" Makellos asked again, giving him a bright smile. An unrequited love was certainly romantic in his eyes. "Have you told him how you feel?"

"Oh, it's quite new," Sigurd said, narrowing his eyes just a bit at Makellos, his lips curving into another smirk.

Makellos opened his mouth to respond before he realized with a bit of consternation that Sigurd was referring to *him*. He cleared his throat, tipping his head down a little so the little black curls at the front of his hair fell forward, giving him a slightly shy look. "Oh. So, were you serious about that kiss?"

Sigurd blinked, then grinned, walking over to the bench where Makellos sat. "Serious if you are."

"And... the others won't be... upset?" Makellos asked.

Sigurd paused, slotting his torso between Makellos' knees, his hands resting on the prince's lower thighs. "I'm not under the illusion that you like me more than any of the others," he said, giving Makellos a strangely serious look. "If what you want is just a bit of fun, whether it's with me, or any of the others, that is okay. I can't speak for anyone but myself, but I'm not the sort to be possessive. I just want to be happy."

Makellos smiled softly. "I... would just like to be happy too." He reached up his hands, not quite sure what he was doing, and placed them a bit awkwardly over Sigurd's bare shoulders to hold him. "Is this all right?"

Sigurd grinned. "Perfect." His hands reached up to cup Makellos' cheeks, and he pressed his mouth to the prince's. It was soft and sweet, and Makellos kissed him back with a bit of caution, since he had never done more than kiss his own mother on the cheek before. Sigurd's hands were rough, but his touch was gentle. After a moment, he pulled back and gave Makellos a smile. "What do you think?"

Makellos let out a breath as a laugh. "I think I like kissing," he said softly.

"Good, then I'll do it again," Sigurd said, leaning in and pressing their lips together, a little firmer this time. Makellos closed his eyes, feeling the sweet touch go through his whole body. His heart gave a happy little hop in his chest, but it also twinged just a little. Sigurd was so kind, and he was more than happy to kiss him, and maybe even go further than that. But it felt strangely unfair. All of the others had been just as kind to him, even Grim with his standoffish attitude. And they weren't here to all talk about it.

"I like you, Sigurd. A lot. But I also like the others as well, and I don't want to hurt anyone. Is it all right if we wait until the others are here to discuss... things?"

"Absolutely," Sigurd said with a small smile. "I know that I am not the only one who has caught feelings for you."

Makellos' sea blue eyes blinked. He knew Sigmund, of course, but were the two brothers the only ones? "Who else?"

Sigurd let out a soft snort of laughter through his nose. "Everyone."

"What?" Makellos demanded in surprise. "No! There's seven of you!"

"What has that got to do with anything?" Sigurd asked with a shrug. "You are beautiful, you are sweet, you are kind. How could anyone *not* like you?"

Makellos let out a single uneasy breath of laughter. "I... have not had anyone who liked me in that way before."

"Perhaps you're just making up for lost time then," Sigurd said with a smirk.

Twelve

That evening, as they all sat around the dining table enjoying roasted meat and vegetables, Hardwic spoke up. "I think we should have some fun tonight, to celebrate Makellos being with us!" he said, giving the prince a cheery grin.

"What did you have in mind?" Bernhardt asked.

"Perhaps some music?" Hardwic suggested. "We haven't had music here for so long."

Dagobert clapped his hands eagerly, giving them all a beaming smile.

"I think that sounds like a marvelous idea," Der said. "Provided the prince is all right with it."

Makellos nodded eagerly, clapping his hands too. "Oh, I should like that very much," he said, his blue eyes lighting up in delight. Even if it was meant for him, the little men had been so kind and worked so hard. If they could have an evening of simple festivities to lighten spirits, especially after the horror of the attack on him the day before, he was sure everyone would benefit. And now that he was aware of it, the prince could see little hints that indicated the miners were each enchanted with him in their own manner. A pink blush, a lowering of the head to gaze at him through lashes, a straightening up of posture. Sigurd's words echoed in his mind again. *"I know that*

I am not the only one who has caught feelings for you. "His heart gave a little flutter in his chest, the beating of butterfly wings against a cool summer breeze.

After dinner was cleared away, Sigmund and Sigurd pulled out a mandolin and a flute respectively, and Hardwic kept the beat with spoons on the bottom of several wooden bowls and a washtub. Bernhardt stepped up and sang a ballad in a beautiful, clear voice that brought tears to Makellos' eyes as he listened to it. Then the music changed to a livelier tune, and Dagobert and Der began to dance.

Dagobert, being the much younger of the two, hopped and spun with an exuberance that Makellos had not seen before. He offered out his hand toward Makellos, his blue eyes lighting up with hope. Makellos smiled back, taking the man's hand and getting to his feet, and they started to dance, a few simple steps as Der, Bernhardt, and a reluctant-seeming Grimwald clapped along. When the dance drew to a close, Dagobert gave Makellos a light tug. Makellos lowered himself to one knee in front of him. Dagobert leaned in, his cheeks and tips of his large ears pink, and he pressed a soft kiss to Makellos' cheek. It was only a quick brush, and Dagobert pulled back, ducking his head like he expected the prince to scold him.

Makellos reached up and touched the spot lightly with his fingertips. He had so rarely been touched in any sort of intimate way, especially on his face, and he could still feel the warmth there. He reached out his hand to lightly touch Dagobert's chin, tipping the young man's face upward so their eyes met. He leaned in and placed a soft, sweet kiss to Dagobert's cheek in return. The little man let out a squeak, his whole body going as red as his hair, and he looked shyly up at Makellos through his lashes as he grinned. The other little men cheered and hooted in laughter, and Dagobert ducked his head again, covering his cheeks with his hands as if to push the blush away.

"Do you know more dances, your highness?" Sigurd asked, and Makellos nodded eagerly.

"Grim is the best dancer of all of us," Hardwic said suddenly with a beaming smile. "I am sure the prince would love to see him dance too."

Grim's dark eyebrows came together in a V on his forehead, glaring at Hardwic. Makellos smiled a little and placed his hands together in a 'please' gesture to him. "I should like very much to see you dance, Grimwald."

"Hmmph," Grim grunted, crossing his arms.

"Oh, don't be such an old warthog," Der said with a roll of his eyes.

"I'm sure the prince is a much better dancer than him anyway," Bernhardt said with a fond smile at Makellos. "Having been raised in a palace and all. Perhaps he can show us how it's done."

Makellos laughed as he straightened up, recognizing what Bernhardt was trying to do. He cast another glance at Grimwald, who merely glowered again. Makellos shrugged and nodded at the musicians.

Hardwic struck up a beat on his makeshift drums, and the brothers joined in after a moment with a jaunty, upbeat tune. Makellos began to move his feet, stepping and hopping, boots pattering lightly across the floor as he danced and spun. He did a complicated little hopping step, and several of the men let out a gasp of delight. "Do that again," Hardwic said eagerly. So, he did.

Dagobert moved up beside Makellos, looking hopeful. Makellos moved his feet in a little hop, and Dagobert imitated it. Makellos did a slight turn, and Dagobert tried to do the same but tripped over his own feet. He went crashing into Der, and they both stumbled, laughing.

"Heh," Grim grunted, getting to his feet. All eyes turned to him. His jaw was firmly set as he stared daggers at Makellos before he did the same hopping step, adding a turn to the end.

Makellos' face lit up with a smile before imitating the movement. The other little men shouted and clapped in delight. Grim glowered a little and did another step, his feet doing a jig on the floor. Makellos did the same step back to him. Grim tapped his feet as he spun and jumped. Makellos did the same. Back and forth they danced, Makellos following Grim step for step. The smaller man was indeed an excellent dancer. His eyebrows seemed to lift as the prince followed his movements until the sour look on his face had faded. His jaw was still tight, but it had lost its harsh set, now tense in concentration. Grim suddenly leaped into the air, rotating twice before he landed again. Makellos took a deep breath and jumped too, but he only made it a turn and a half, and he tripped over his own feet as he landed, Bernhardt and Dagobert having to help steady him as everyone laughed and cheered. Der slapped Grim on the back jovially, and the dark-eyed man looked very pleased with himself. But the self-satisfied smile he turned on the prince was just a bit warmer than his usual cold detachment.

Afterward, Makellos collapsed to the floor in a gale of laughter, clapping his hands. "That was marvelous! You are such great musicians and wonderful dancers."

"When there's not a lot to amuse yourself, you do what you can," Sigurd said as he tucked his flute away in its box and put it on the shelf.

"And you are quite the dancer yourself," Bernhardt added, giving Makellos a bright smile.

"Thank you," Makellos said, picking himself up off the floor. All eyes were on him right now, and he realized that this might be a grand opportunity to address them all when they were all in such high spirits. He took a deep breath and squared his shoulders, as he had been taught to do when addressing people. "I did wish to speak with all of you," he said, trying to put confidence into his tone despite his stomach flipping inside of him.

Seven pairs of eyes watched him, and Makellos put on his most charming smile. "First, I want to thank you all so much for allowing me to stay in your home and become part of your little family. You have all been so kind, and I can never repay that kindness."

Murmurs went around as the little men thanked him in return or batted away his concern of compensation. Makellos took another breath and continued on. "It has come to my attention that more than one of you might be fond of me, in a way that goes beyond simple friendship."

That sent a rustle around the room, and Sigmund shot his brother a reproachful look. "You told him, didn't you?"

"He dragged it out of me," Sigurd said with a smug smile.

Makellos laughed softly as several others gave Sigurd annoyed looks. "Please, do not be upset with him. I am glad to finally know. If any relationships are to develop, I want to be aware of how each of you feel. It is not fair to burden you with secret longings that cannot be expressed."

"We are quite used to navigating each other," Bernhardt said kindly. "It is *you* we are concerned about, your highness. Your feelings are important too, and none of us wish to be a cause of pain or confusion for you."

Heads nodded in agreement, and Makellos felt his twisting stomach calm just a little at the reassurance. "I do appreciate that, more than I can say," he said. "I just don't want you to think that I favor any one of you above the other. You all have become so dear to me in your own unique ways, I don't know how I would ever be able to choose."

Glances were exchanged between several of the men before Sigmund turned to him with a small smirk. "Who says you have to choose?"

Makellos blinked. "What do you mean?"

"I mean, we're all adults here. We, as in, us," he indicated the other miners around the table, "are all comfortable with one another in many aspects, including navigating relationships. There are no rules that say you must share your love or your bed with only one person."

The words bounced around in his head for a few moments before Makellos was able to fully process them. And then he realized Sigmund was right. A pairing between two people was the most common form of love, but that did not mean it was the only option. And here, he was not a prince, expected to make a match for sake of treaty or power. Here, he was just Makellos. Just Snow White. He could make his own decisions, something he did not get to do often in the palace.

"Would you really be all right with that?" he asked, glancing around the room at the seven faces of the men he treasured so dearly. "I don't see how I could ever only share my heart with one of you."

Dagobert smiled shyly at him. "I like you," he said softly.

Makellos felt warmth surge inside of him. "I like you too, Dagobert."

Everyone smiled at that. Even Grim's mouth quirked up at the edges just a bit.

"I admit that my experiences in the bedroom have been... very limited," Makellos said, his cheeks going pink. "Or, rather, non-existent." He ducked his head, realizing how personal he was getting. "I don't know if that influences any of you in some way."

"As in, if any of us are uncomfortable with a virgin?" Bernhardt said, not unkindly.

"Well, yes. For whatever reason, really," Makellos said. "I do not wish to be a burden upon any of you."

"Stop that," Grim scolded, his tone sharp, and Makellos jumped. "We've all been there at one point or another. Ain't no reason to be ashamed of inexperience. The question is, how do you feel about it?"

"What do you mean?" Makellos asked softly.

"I don't know, you're a prince. Do you have some sort of romantic fairy tale idea of what your first time would be like or who you want it to be with?" Grim asked, his eyebrows coming to a single point in the middle of his forehead as he stared almost sternly at Makellos.

"Oh, I..." Makellos flushed again, swallowing hard as he looked around the table. "No, I don't suppose that I do. I know some people find it special and only want to share it with one specific person, someone they really love. But I don't know how I would ever choose between all of you for that either. As much as you say you're all right with my having individual relationships, I do feel like that's a bit unfair. You have all been so wonderful to me, and I'd hate for anyone to feel like they are not being included or having to wait on my affections."

"Your fairness reflects your inner beauty yet again," said Hardwic with a smile.

"Oh, here's an idea," said Sigmund, holding up his hand. "I for one would love to suck that gorgeous cock of yours. Why don't we come together, and then... come together?" He wiggled his eyebrows.

Makellos felt the blush paint his face once more. "What do you mean?" he asked. Was Sigmund really suggesting that he take them all as his lovers in bed at once?

"You mean all of us at the same time?" Hardwic said.

"Well, alternate some, obviously," Sigmund said. "Only so many hands and holes and everything."

"Sigmund!" Der scolded, his own cheeks bright pink spots.

"What? It's just a suggestion," Sigmund said, holding up his hands. "Obviously it's entirely up to the prince."

Makellos felt his heart start to race in his chest as all eyes turned to him. He suddenly felt like he had when Hans had trapped him against that boulder in the woods, nowhere to run, waiting for the blow to fall. But this time, the blow was his choice. And it was not a knife coming for his heart. And, to his surprise, he realized his cock was growing hard inside of his breeches, throbbing a little at the idea. "Would you... all be patient with me?" he asked, the blush still coloring his cheeks.

A chorus of 'yes' and 'of course' met him, smiles all around from the men who watched him fondly. "I don't think any of us would expect you to really be good at anything to start," Bernhardt said, his voice kind.

"In fact, I'm all for the prince just relaxing and letting us pleasure him into oblivion," Sigurd said, his voice playful and his smile wicked as he turned his eyes to Makellos.

"Oh, I like that idea," Sigmund said, giving his brother a nudge.

"Are... *you* all right with that?" Makellos asked, glancing between them all. "I do not wish for my participation to not be enjoyable."

"Oh, we'll enjoy you, don't worry," said Grim a bit salaciously, to the surprise of everyone. His dark eyebrows lifted as he gazed around at the others all staring at him. "What?"

Even grumpy old Grimwald was excited by this plan, Makellos thought. "All right," he said, sweeping his sunshine smile around the room. "I would be honored to take you all to bed with me."

"All right," Sigmund said eagerly, already rising to his feet.

"Now now," Doc said, holding up his hand. "The prince decides when he wants to do it."

Makellos felt his heart flutter again. "You all are so very kind. I see no reason to delay it. But I do admit I'm a little nervous."

"That's all right," Sigurd said with a reassuring smile. "Whatever we can do to make you more comfortable."

"Here's an idea, if it appeals to you, your highness," said Bernhardt, rubbing a hand over his beard. "What if we blindfold you? Then you can touch and taste and do whatever you'd like without knowing to whom the attention is being lavished."

"Oh, how very devious of you, Bern," said Grim with a snort.

"But it would be entirely fair," Der said thoughtfully. "Provided, of course, the prince is all right with that."

All eyes suddenly turned to Makellos again, and he felt the heat burn in his face even as a smile tugged the corners of his lips upward.

"Yes," he said softly, his cock now fully at attention in his breeches, apparently very on board with this new plan.

"Excellent," said Der with a clap of his hands. "I've got a lovely silk scarf I've been saving that will do quite nicely as a blindfold and should be quite comfortable."

"Getting all fancy on us, doc," Sigurd teased.

"And we all understand, no means no," Hardwic added, his usual cheerful face strangely serious. "Stop is stop. We do not ever wish to hurt you, your highness. We want you to feel safe in our hands."

"I do. I trust you all," Makellos said softly. He cleared his throat, suddenly feeling a little nervousness in the pit of his stomach. "But would you...?" His voice trailed off.

All seven of the little men leaned in toward him. "What?" asked Hardwic and Der at the same time.

"Would you all please call me Snow? I would like to forget that I am a prince for while."

Another chorus of agreements and 'still a silly name' from Grim met him, and Snow beamed. "Thank you. How... shall we do this?"

"Would you like to get undressed first?" Hardwic asked.

"I suppose I am not very used to being naked around other people," Makellos said with a laugh.

"It's quite refreshing sometimes," said Hardwic. "Especially here with each other, where we don't get judged for our bodies."

Makellos nodded. Perhaps once he was naked, he would feel a little less unsure of this whole thing. He took off his waistcoat, then his shirtsleeves, baring his torso. Several whoops and wolf-whistles went up, and he ducked his head shyly. "I'm certain it's not that incredible."

"You really are the fairest in the land," Bernhardt said appreciatively, and the others murmured their assent.

Makellos blushed, setting the clothes aside, then toed off his boots, and lastly, reached to undo his breeches. He took a deep breath as he finished undoing the fastenings, and then slid them slowly down his legs. Dagobert reached out and took them from him with a smile, and Makellos gave him a slightly nervous one in return. He resisted the urge to cover himself, instead straightening his back as he had always been taught a prince should, aware that his cock was standing fully at attention as well between his legs.

"Damn, we better get this going, or I'm not going to last long enough," said Sigmund with a flirty wink at Makellos. The prince laughed softly, which seemed to break the tension inside of him. For all of his mother's talk of beauty and being the definition of perfection, he had never really considered himself to be the object of anyone's sexual attraction.

"We're going to make you feel so good," Sigurd purred.

Makellos flushed. "I know you will."

Der moved over to the dresser, rooting around for a moment, before he pulled put a long, red silk scarf that shimmered in the light from the lantern. Makellos hesitated for only a moment before he lowered himself to his knees so that Der could put the blindfold on him. It was whisper-soft as it slipped over his eyes. Der wound it several times around his head until Makellos could see nothing at all. "Comfortable?"

"Very," he said softly, to laughs from the little men. Der tied it at the back of his head, and Makellos adjusted his hair as he heard the men move around him. From the rustle, it sounded like everyone was removing their clothing, and his breath hitched a little in anticipation. Between his knees, his cock gave a hopeful twitch. What would it be like, to have all of those hands on him? Touching him in places no one else had touched before? With his eyes covered, he suddenly became aware of a host of other sensations. The creak of the floorboard beneath his knees, the cool wood on his skin. He could feel and hear the men walking around near him, though he had no idea what they might be doing, and goosebumps rose on his skin.

He was more aware of scent now too. He could smell the warm bodies around him, a mix of manly sweat, sawdust, an earthy smell that he assumed was what the mines smelled like. He could tell each of the men had their own unique scent, even if it wasn't overt, and his mind guessed who passed near him.

A hand landed on his shoulder, the sudden touch and the sensation of a calloused palm on his bare skin making him jump. "Sorry," said Der. "Here now, on your feet, we'll take you to the bed."

Makellos pushed himself up to his feet, suddenly very aware, despite not being able to see it, that the movement gave a good view of his naked form. "We're going to touch you now," said Der, and several warm hands of various sizes and softness were placed upon his skin, mostly his hips and lower back, giving him a gentle steer in the direction of the bed, like guiding a ship into a harbor. He took a few tentative steps before feeling more confident with the hands to guide him.

"Lie down on the bed, on your right," said Der. "We'll help you."

Makellos reached next to him and found the edge of the bed, lowering himself down and then sliding back toward the center of it. The bedframes creaked softly as he felt some of the men climb on as well, hands guiding him into position and placing a pillow beneath his head. He took a deep breath, his legs demurely closed, unsure what he should be doing.

He felt someone over him, blocking out the light even if he couldn't see it, and then a pair of soft lips pressed to his own. He let out a slightly surprised sound, but he quickly kissed back. Warmth gathered around him on all sides as the little men surrounded him. A hand slid over his shin. Another slid up his hip. Someone ran their fingers through his hair. Another kiss pressed to his lips, different than the first, and another set of lips brushed over the pale column of his neck. He gasped as more hands and lips joined in the exploration of him, smoothing over his skin, massaging his muscles under tough, strong fingers. Lips and even tongues brushed over him, tickling his sides and making him laugh and squirm. Someone took one of his fingers into their mouth and began to slowly suck on it, teasing his tongue over the soft pad of Makellos' fingertip.

A tongue brushed his earlobe. A set of lips found the soft spot just above one of his hip bones and gave it a light nip before suckling soothingly over the spot. Hands rubbed over his feet, massaging the balls of them and in between each toe, before a kiss was pressed to the top of his foot, making it twitch. He had no idea anymore who was touching him, and that was strangely freeing. Makellos allowed himself to relax and just focus on the sensations sweeping over him. Each hand felt different, but all felt so good, so kind and warm on his flesh. None of them had even touched between his legs yet, despite his hard cock begging for attention, but he reminded himself there was no reason to rush. They had all night if they wanted.

Another kiss pressed to his lips, then trailed kisses down his jaw to his neck as someone else kissed him too. Makellos moaned before realizing how wanton and needy that sounded, and he clapped his hand to his mouth as a blush colored his cheeks bright pink.

A hand, a very small one that he thought was Bernhardt's, gently pulled his hand away from his mouth. "No one to hear you but us," he said gently. "And we want to hear you." And then he pressed kisses to Makellos' palm.

"I... I am not used to sharing my passions," the prince said, almost feeling guilty at how innocent and naïve he must sound.

"Just do or say whatever feels right," said Sigurd in his ear before giving it a light nip with his teeth. Makellos squeaked, which prompted several bouts of laughter, but the hands and lips on him suddenly became much firmer, less exploratory and more possessive. A hand suddenly slid between his legs, cupping his balls, and he mewled a sound he didn't think he had ever made before. Someone else brushed several fingers up and down his straining cock before wrapping around it and beginning to stroke up and down.

His cock gave a pleading twitch, and he could feel slickness leaking from the head to help the stroking hand. The hand holding his balls slid lower, pressing against the sensitive skin behind them before creeping lower still, brushing ever so lightly between the cheeks of his pert ass. He flushed, the back of one hand going self-consciously to his face. He heard the chiding click of a tongue, and he dropped it again. "Good boy, Snow," cooed Der.

He had been called 'good boy' before by his tutors or nursemaids, but never in a way that sent heat coursing through his veins like fire. His cock gave an eager pulse, and he let out a soft whimper.

"I think he likes being our good boy," Sigmund said. "Do you, Snow?"

"I... I do," Makellos, no, Snow, said. He wanted to be a good boy. He wanted those sweet kisses and touches and hands all over him, making his skin tingle and heat blossom inside of him like a flower stretching up toward the sun. "I want to be so good for all of you."

"Mmm, I think he's ready for more," said Hardwic.

Snow's heartbeat picked up in his chest at that. More. This already felt better than anything in the world ever had, his blood singing in his veins, his limbs heavy, his cock quivering in the hand of whomever held him. "Yes," he said softly, groping out his fingers until he found skin, not sure whom he was touching but just wanting the reassuring warmth. "I want more."

"Then spread your legs, dear Snow," said Der. Snow felt his cheeks heat, but he obediently slid his knees apart, opening himself up for them to see. Several hands traced down the backs of his thighs, then up to gently squeeze at the globes of his smooth ass. He tensed a little.

"All right?" asked someone he thought was Sigurd.

"Yes," Snow breathed softly, giving a smile to the darkness. "I'm just not used to... being touched like that."

There were soft but kind laughs from around him, and someone leaned in to kiss his lips, hands cupping his jaw on either side to hold him there. A warm, wet tongue brushed over his lower lip, then teased carefully between them. Snow opened his mouth and let the tongue sweep inside. His own tongue inched out to shyly brush back, eliciting a moan from whomever was kissing him. He thought it might be Dagobert, but he wasn't entirely sure. Their tongue tangled together, exploratory at first. Snow moaned softly, then gasped against the mouth as someone, no, two someones, slid up by his legs and lifted them off the bed. A moment later, they were pushed wider, and his knees draped over what felt like the shoulders of two different men, spreading him obscenely wide and open. He let out a gasp against the mouth that kissed him, but the tongue continued to plunder his lips and inside of his mouth, and he moaned louder, his hands sliding up to hold the soft, hairless cheeks of the man kissing him. Dagobert, he confirmed.

Snow jumped as someone pulled his ass cheeks gently apart and blew a soft, cool breath onto his virgin hole. He tried to relax, but he jumped again as he felt the brush of facial hair against his thighs, and then the probe of something soft and wet against his hole that flicked up and down. He realized after a moment that it was a tongue, and his breath hitched eagerly. Dagobert pulled back from Snow's lips and began to press kisses down his neck to his chest.

The tongue between his legs flickered up and down over his hole, then around in a circle. He mewled and tried hard not to squirm, but he gave up that idea very quickly when someone straddled themselves backward across his chest, then leaned down and took his cock into their mouth. He cried out in pleasure as that sweet, hot mouth closed over the head of his cock and sucked while the tongue circled and probed over his hole. He let the shoulders supporting his legs take his weight, moaning eagerly at the doubled pleasure of the tongue brushing his hole while the mouth sealed around his cock.

The tongue probed harder, so slick and warm, and Snow gasped as he felt it slip inside of him, past the initial tightness at his hole, and then deeper inside his virgin passage. "Oh," he gasped, hands gripping the pillow by his head. The tongue slid in and out as the mouth over his cock began to slide further down, then up again, starting up a slow rhythm. He already felt pleasure pooling in his lower body, and they had only just begun. He moaned, then yelped and nearly shot up off of the bed when two tongues brushed over his nipples, swirling around them playfully. He collapsed back down with a broken cry of bliss.

A hand suddenly touched his, and he let it guide him off the pillow and over to someone's fully erect cock, large and hot in his hand. He moaned and began to explore it with his fingertips, sliding down its length, down the veiny underside, to the balls there that he cupped and rolled cautiously in his hand, making soft whimpering noises as someone nipped one of his nipples and then lapped over it soothingly. There was so much sensation, his body quivered with it, wanting to feel it all but yet focus on only one at a time.

His body tensed as the desire built into a growing need, his balls pulling up tight as he made a soft pleading that he wasn't even sure was actually words before he spilled himself with a cry into the mouth sucking on him. The movement didn't stop, the lips there still curling around him as they sucked him, getting every last drop of his seed from the tip of his cock, the tongue inside of him still thrusting and swirling until he thought he might scream from the stimulation that sent little jolts of lightning through his body.

And then both of the mouths pulled away, as did the ones on his nipples, leaving him with the cock in his hand and his legs still spread and bent wide where they rested on shoulders. There was a rustling whisper, and then suddenly everyone had pulled away from him, his legs on the bed once more. He found himself alone, trying not to squirm as his hole suddenly felt very empty, and his whole body chilled. There were some footfalls, and then a few whispers from off to his right, which sounded like all of them were gathered together. He swallowed, trying to listen in to find out what his fate might be, but he couldn't make out any of the words. Then someone, he was pretty sure it was Sigmund, leaned down to whisper in his ear. "We're going to let you choose, fairest. We're going to stand around the bed, and you point to which of us you want to pop that sweet virgin cherry of yours."

Snow gasped softly, his heart fluttering in his chest at both the intrigue of not knowing who his choice would be, and the thought of someone fucking him for the first time. He supposed this was the fairest way to decide, as each of them had a one in seven chance of being selected. "Wh... what about the rest of you?" he breathed out.

"Oh, don't worry," said a different voice that he thought was Bernhardt. "We'll all have a chance at one time or another."

"And you can please us in so many other ways too," said what sounded like Hardwic. "But first, we want you to enjoy your first fucking."

Snow wasn't sure why that made him blush beneath his blindfold. Perhaps just because it came from Hardwic's mouth. "All right," he said, casting a smile in their direction.

"Do you want to know who your choice is after you pick?" asked Der.

Snow thought about it for a moment. "No," he said softly. "Don't tell me unless I ask."

"Very well," Der said with a chuckle. "We'll stand around the bed, and you point."

Snow relaxed down against the bed as best he could, his heart still beating rapidly in his chest like a bird beating against its cage to escape. He wasn't sure why he was nervous, but he was sure that everything would be fine. All of them cared about him and his feelings, and if something was wrong, he was sure they would speak up. He heard the soft patter of bare feet on the floorboards of the room and did his best to listen for the silence when they were all in place. He sat up, taking a deep breath. He turned his head over his shoulder, then the other way, then in front of him. He couldn't even see any light around his blindfold, so he really was just taking a random guess. He lifted his left hand and pointed to an angle behind him.

There was a soft giggle and a few breaths, and then he felt and heard all of them approach the bed around him. "Was that all right?" he asked, hoping he had not hurt any of their feelings by not selecting them, even though it was not something he had intentionally done.

"Yes," said a voice next to him that sounded like Hardwic. "Just relax, we're all going to take care of you."

Snow nodded and settled back against the bed again. He felt multiple men slide onto the bed next to him, and one between his spread knees. He heard the pop of a stopper being undone, which made him jump just a little.

Hardwic's hand, or at least, he assumed that from where the voice had come a moment ago, rested gently on his shoulder, giving him a reassuring rub. "Just oil. Der's special concoction."

That made him feel a little better, for he trusted Der's work, and the fact that they were looking out to ensure they did not hurt him. He reached up a hand to press lightly onto Hardwic's on his shoulder. "Will the rest of you put your hands on me?" he asked, keeping the request soft and sweet.

"Of course," Hardwic said, and there were suddenly hands resting all over him. More than six, so he assumed that some of them were using both hands. But all of them were warm, stroking and massaging and gently circling his skin, on his shoulders, chest, hips, arms, legs. Everywhere there was a warm, calloused hand, some rougher, some larger or smaller, but all of them soothing. Makellos let out a soft, contented sound. If he had not been blindfolded, he would have just closed his eyes and let the touches lull him into a sort of stupor.

A finger slid between his legs, brushing over his hole, and he did not jump this time, only took a deep breath and let it out. The finger pressed at his hole, much firmer and less flexible than a tongue, and he gasped when the slick digit pushed past the first tight ring of muscle and inside of him. It was not a small finger, and the stretch of his virgin passage around it made him whimper softly. Hands tenderly caressed his hair and his cheek. "Breathe," came a voice from his right side that he was pretty sure was Der.

So, he did, focusing on the soothing hands all over him, letting himself relax as much as he could. While the finger was large and rough, the man attached to it was being quite gentle, he could tell, not pushing too hard but also not so lightly that he didn't make progress in sliding the finger all the way inside of him. It made a curling motion that made his breath hitch and his hips buck upward just a bit. The hands on him stroked over his skin, lighting him up like a bonfire. Fingers stroked his hair, someone kissed his lips, someone else nibbled at his neck. The finger inside of him swirled and moved around inside of him before he felt a second fingertip at his hole, seeking entry. He let out a breath, lifting his knees a little higher, and the second finger slid in beside the first. He moaned, his eyelashes fluttering behind his blindfold.

"All right?" prompted Der.

"Yes," Snow murmured. The fingers inside of him curled and twisted gently, sending a cavalcade of sensation through him, and he writhed under all of the touches. Even this felt so incredible, he could scarcely breathe.

Gradually a third finger, coated extra liberally with oil, slid inside of him, making him give a soft whimper of discomfort. Multiple hands and voices reassured him that he was doing so well, that he was such a good boy, to keep breathing, they weren't going to leave him. He didn't think he could feel as full as he did with three fingers inside of him, but the feeling gradually faded into a pleasurable stretch, and he felt himself suddenly physically relax, the tension he didn't know he had been holding easing away.

"There you go, good boy," said a voice from the man between his knees. It was surprisingly gentle, because he was almost sure it was Grimwald. He became keenly aware of the other hands on him, trying to figure out who they were, and while he was not completely sure on all of them, he was sure now that Grim was the one in front of him. That made him warm all over. He had chosen randomly, but the fact that it was Grim just felt right somehow.

After another few minutes of the fingers moving inside of him, he felt a kiss on his inner thigh, and Der said, "Are you ready to try the real thing?"

Snow let out a breath and nodded. "Yes. Please."

Grim's fingers slid out of him, and he moaned softly at the loss of sensation. He tried to stay relaxed, made easier by all of the hands on him, and kisses that brushed over his body. He heard the slick sound of oil on skin, and then Grim was back between his knees. Something large, he assumed the head of Grim's cock, pressed against his hole, and Snow exhaled again. The head slid in with a bit of a burn in the stretch, and Snow tensed a little. Hands petted and caressed him, lips brushed over his face, his chest, his hair. He clung to those sensations as Grim slid, slowly and smoothly, deep inside of him, deeper than anything had ever been. His eyes watered a little behind the blindfold, but he still smiled. "Oh," he breathed. "Yes..."

It felt tight, but there was no pain as Grim's hips began to move, slowly, rocking back and forth into him, never quite pulling out. Snow moaned, lifting his knees a little further, which helped the slide, and the angle felt even better. The head of Grim's cock suddenly pressed against something inside of him that sent heat spiking through his veins like a lit match, and Snow bucked up in surprise with a soft yelp. Several laughs around him soothed him. "There you go," Grim purred, his voice still that soothing gentleness. "That's a good boy, Snow. Just relax and let Daddy make you feel so good."

The movements that followed that left Snow gasping for breath. He caught the hand of one of the men and held it tight, the other hands still stroking his skin and raining kisses upon him. Fingers pinched at his pink nipples, rolling and flicking them back and forth. A slick hand grabbed his cock and began to stroke in time with the thrusts from Grim's hips, and Snow knew he wasn't going to last much longer. He let out a sound that was half nonsense pleading, half a sob, as his back arched up, heat flooding his body as spilled himself over the stroking hands. The stimulation continued as Grim thrust several more times between his legs into his tight heat before he ground against Snow with a soft shout of pleasure. Snow could vaguely hear sounds around him, sounds of kisses and stroking, and someone let out a gasping grunt. He realized that the little miners were not only pleasuring him, but also either themselves or others, and his heart gave a little leap of happiness. He wanted everyone to feel pleasure like he did, and the fact that they were brought to fulfillment from watching him sent another thrill through his body.

Grim on top of him was heavy and comforting, sinewy muscles under warm skin, each brush of which made him tingle all over. Still with only darkness for vison, Snow panted for a few moments before he began to relax again, settling down into the mattress, under the many hands that rested on him now.

He realized as his mind slowly drifted back down to earth that he had started to cry. The blindfold, wet with tears, was carefully pulled off his head and away from his hair, soothing hands stroking his cheeks. He squinted his eyes open to see seven concerned faces gazing back at him. "Are you all right, Snow?" asked Hardwic, clutching his hand and giving the back of it a kiss.

"Did I hurt you?" Grimwald asked worried, stroking a large hand up Snow's thigh.

"What can we do?" asked Sigurd.

Snow panted softly as his body relaxed into what he thought melting butter must feel like. "I'm all right. It was wonderful," he said, his sky-blue eyes flicking from one man to the next. "It was perfect, and I am so glad I was able to share it with all of you."

"We are too," said Der, stroking his cheek lightly. "Thank you for giving us this honor."

Snow chuckled softly as the little men all settled around him on the bed, still holding his hands, stroking his hair, touching his chest and legs to connect them all with him at the center. "I am the one who is honored," he said. "I have found in you the most amazing, strong men who have endured so much. My true friends, my dear lovers, each and every one of you. No man has ever been as lucky as I."

There were several soft sighs of pleasure, pink blushes, and various happy smiles around when Dagobert suddenly spoke up. "We love you, Snow." All heads turned to look at Dagobert in surprise before they then turned to the prince beneath them.

Snow took each of their hands and placed them on his chest, just above his heart, then rested his own over top of them. "And I love all of you. With every beat of my heart."

Thirteen

The nights were growing colder, but the little cottage was full of laughter and warmth. In the morning, Snow kissed each of the men goodbye before they headed off to the mines to work. There was still much to be done around the cottage. Bernhardt taught him how to sew; he used to help make and maintain the costumes for his acting troupe. They spent the afternoon in front of the fire, patching holes in warm clothing that would be needed for winter as Bernhardt recounted many a tale of his travels throughout the lands. He had traveled much farther than anyone Snow had ever known, and his eyes took on a faraway look when he reminisced about those days.

"I know you were an actor, and Der was an apothecary," Snow said thoughtfully. "Sigurd and Sigmund were carpenters. Was Grimwald a woodcutter by trade?"

"Indeed, he was," said Bernhardt.

"And Dagobert was just a child when he was taken to the mines. What about Hardwic?"

"What about him?" Bernhardt asked, his eyes on his stitches.

"What did he do for work? I know he had a wife and daughter, but that is all that he has said about his past."

Bernhardt chuckled softly. "Well, to be honest, none of us are entirely sure what he used to do. He's never told us."

"Wait. In twenty-two years, he has never mentioned what his life was like before coming to the mines?" Snow asked in surprise.

"Oh, we have asked him, of course," Bernhardt said thoughtfully. "But he's never given us an answer."

Snow wondered what the rotund little man could have done that he did not want to talk about his past. Hardwic was always so cheerful and bright. But instead, he asked, "What about you? Would you go back to being an actor if you could?"

Bernhardt got that faraway look in his eyes again, the skin around them crinkling into a lifetime of lines. "You know, lad, I've given it thought. I didn't ever expect our lot to change. I'm an old man now, and I expected that I would die in those mines. But perhaps one day, things might be different." He gave Snow a bright smile that lit up his aged face. "I don't think I'd travel again. After twenty-two years, the others, they've become my family. I wouldn't want to leave them, perhaps never to return. I'd like to stay close. But as to returning to the stage, well, that I could certainly do at any age."

"Would you perform something for me?" Snow asked. "You sang so beautifully last night."

Bernhardt's gray eyes lit from within as though a lantern had flared to life behind them. He straightened in his chair, suddenly shedding the fatigue of the last twenty-odd years, his body taking on the countenance of a man half his age. He held up his sewing needle in front of him and began to recite a monologue that Snow had never heard before, but it was so filled with drama and tragedy that it brought tears to his eyes as he watched the little man become what he had been before the Queen destroyed it. At the end, Bernhardt gave a little bow, and Snow burst into applause.

"That was wonderful!" he exclaimed before leaning in to give Bernhardt a fond kiss.

"Thank you," Bernhardt said, his face uncharacteristically red from the kiss and the praise. "It has been a long time since I've done that. But it felt good."

"You did it so beautifully," Snow said. "I am honored that you showed me your talent."

Bernhardt had a bright smile on his face for the rest of the afternoon.

Snow wasn't sure what woke him as he lay in the darkness, warm under blankets and multiple bodies pressed against him. He heard a soft creak from the floorboards and realized that someone was up and had just walked out into the main room. He did a quick count in his head, trying to find everyone around him in the darkness. It was definitely one of the little men, and he thought it was one of the brothers. He supposed he didn't necessarily need to get up and check, but curiosity got the better of him. He had to wiggle carefully to get the blanket off of him. Next to him, Dagobert rolled over and mumbled something incomprehensible, but the movement allowed Snow to slide the blanket down. Extricating himself from the pile of bodies was another task. He had to lift up several arms to get them off of him, but luckily, no one awakened from his gentle touches. He slipped off the large bed, his bare feet landing on the cold wooden floor.

He tried to keep his steps light on the creaky wooden boards as he crossed over in just the moonlight. He peered into the main room and found Sigmund sitting on one of the benches, fully dressed, with a cup of water. He slowly approached him, letting his steps grow a little louder so he did not startle the man. "Hello," he said.

Sigmund looked up at him in surprise. "Hi. Sorry, did I wake you?"

"No," Snow said, giving him a soft smile. "I'm just a light sleeper sometimes. You aren't tired?"

"Nope, not sleepy at all," Sigmund said, taking a sip of the water. "On the days when it's my turn to stay home, I generally don't sleep well leading into it. So, I get up early to go hunting."

"May I sit with you until you leave?" Snow asked, gesturing to the bench next to him.

"Of course." Sigmund waved his hand, and Snow sat. He had spent significant time with Sigurd, but not with Sigmund beyond their flirting. He wanted to get to know him better, as he did with all of the little men.

"Sigurd told me about your fiancé," he said softly.

"Yes, he told me," Sigmund said, fiddling with the handle of his cup.

"I'm so very sorry."

"It's all right," Sigmund said, not meeting his eyes. "I am rather glad we were not married when they came for me. Who knows what they might have done?"

"Do you think about where he might be now?"

"Every day," Sigmund said, looking up at Snow, his hazel eyes much more somber than Snow had ever seen him.

"Perhaps, one day, you can find him again," Snow said softly.

Sigmund's smile was small. "It's been twenty-two years. I don't expect him to be waiting on a wish for that long. He had a life to live and no reason to think that I might come back. I just hope he is happy, wherever things may have taken him."

"I want to help all of you," Snow said softly, reaching out to place a hand on Sigmund's shoulder. "I don't know yet what I can do, but what was done to all of you was monstrous."

"You have a good heart, Snow," Sigmund said, glancing down at the hand on his shoulder before taking the hand and squeezing it lightly. "Just by being here, you've brought light back into this dreary place."

Snow smiled and held Sigmund's hand with both of his. "You all have been so kind to me, when you had every reason not to be. I can never thank you enough for that."

Sigmund grinned back at him. "Our lives may have gone to shit because of the Queen, but that doesn't mean we're already dead, right?"

"That's right," Snow said. "And I'm not dead either. I'll find some way to help you all, and some way to repay your kindness."

"Well, you could always suck my cock," Sigmund said lightly, giving Snow a playful wink, the old Sigmund he knew returning.

Snow blinked. He knew Sigmund was teasing. But he had never done that before, and the idea of it intrigued him, especially with the thrill of being caught by the other six in the next room. "Maybe I shall," he said before sliding off the bench and crawling beneath the dining table.

"What? Shit, Snow, I was just joking," Sigmund said quickly, trying to push himself back from the table, but Snow reached up and placed his hands on Sigmund's knees. It was dark under the table, only moonlight from the windows illuminating the room. It was almost like being in a warm, dark cave. And he felt safe. Protected. Nothing would happen to him here in the darkness. He squeezed Sigmund's knees lightly.

"I know you were, but I would like to try. If that's all right with you."

Sigmund glanced down at him under the table, before a wicked grin spread across his face. "Well, you *do* look absolutely gorgeous on your knees like that, Snow White."

Snow's face went pink at the praise. He slid his hands up Sigmund's thighs to trace over the front of his loose breeches. He could feel the man's cock, already slightly hard, under the fabric, and he stroked over it with his hands. He fumbled with the laces closing them, then laughed when all he did was catch his fingers in them. "Perhaps you should do this part."

Sigmund chuckled and undid the fastenings, then reached in and pulled out his cock, already half-hard. Snow couldn't see it very well in the darkness of the room, but he could see enough to know he wanted it. He leaned in, brushing his tongue up the underside of the head, giving it an experimental lick. Sigmund sighed softly, the hand not holding his cock for Snow sliding down to stroke through the dark strands of the prince's hair.

Snow let his tongue trace up and down, exploring it until the cock stood hard and firm in front of him. He rested one hand on Sigmund's knee, the other sliding down to hold the base of the cock as he cautiously slid his mouth down, taking in first just the head, giving it a hesitant suck. Sigmund moaned softly, his fingers pressing harder into Snow's hair. Encouraged, Snow did it again, letting his tongue trace a little awkwardly up and down and swirl all around. He wasn't quite sure what he was doing, but it seemed that Sigmund was enjoying the movements. Confidence was key, he was sure, so he put all his effort into the movements, making them firm and eager, even if they were a bit sloppy.

He carefully slid his mouth down until his lips met his own hand where he gripped the base so he didn't go too far and choke himself. With practice, he knew he'd be able to take more, but for his first time, he didn't want to push himself too far. He moaned softly around the cock, letting his tongue trace over the head again. "Good boy, Snow, that's it," Sigmund purred, stroking his hair. Encouraged, Snow bobbed his head up and down, like he had felt Sigmund do to him the other morning. It took a few tries before he found a good angle and rhythm that he liked, and his mouth watered more than he expected, but he decided that he liked this, giving pleasure to someone with his mouth, especially when Sigmund let out a sound that was half gasp, half growl. "Fuck yeah, beautiful, just like that."

Snow bobbed his head up and down, letting his hand slide up and down the spit-slick shaft too for extra stimulation. He could taste the salty beads forming at the tip of Sigmund's cock, and he paused to run his tongue over it and swallow them before going back to bobbing his head. His jaw was a little tired, not used to this sort of motion, but he was not about to stop. The little men had given him so much pleasure the other day, he wanted to return the favor as much as he could, and the sounds Sigmund was making were like music to his ears.

Moving his tongue around to tease as his head bobbed was becoming easier, and he felt little surges under his fingers wrapped around Sigmund's shaft. The man's fingers tightened in his hair a little. "Gonna... come, Snow..." he warned. Snow eagerly kept up the movement, trying to encourage Sigmund with his hand and mouth. He wanted to bring the man to his release, to bring him pleasure and make him feel as good as everyone made him feel. Sigmund let out a breathy little shout that sounded much louder in the silence of the cottage than it probably was, and he spilled his passion into Snow's mouth.

He wasn't quite sure what he had expected, but feeling Sigmund's cock throb and pulse in between his lips made Snow's heart do a little dance inside of him. But he choked trying to swallow it down, not quite prepared for it, and most of it dripped from his mouth. He swiped at it with his hand and then brushed it over his breeches, the mess fading away instantly as he slowly drew back from Sigmund under the table and swallowed thickly again.

Sigmund panted softly, then reached down to pull Snow forward. Snow followed and let him guide him out from under the table and to his feet again. Sigmund grinned. "My turn." He pushed Snow back until the young man was sitting on the edge of the dining table, his fingers deftly undoing his breeches. He was much faster and efficient than Snow had been, and his own cock was down Sigmund's throat almost before Snow realized what was happening. He let out a gasp, his hands flying to the little man's hair, holding onto it. Sigmund wrapped his arms around Snow's lower back and pulled him close so his face was practically mashed against Snow's lower stomach, sucking and licking at his cock like a starving man served a gourmet meal.

He mewled softly, Sigmund's throat swallowing him expertly, and he knew he wasn't going to last long anyway. He panted and groaned, his fingers clawing lightly at Sigmund's hair, his head tipped back and eyes half-lidded in pleasure. He barely noticed when someone entered from the bedroom, until he heard Grim's soft chuckle, "Well, good morning. Got your breakfast already, I see."

Sigmund made a rude gesture at Grim but didn't stop what he was doing. Snow felt a slightly embarrassed blush color his face, but he forced himself to stay still and let Sigmund continue to pleasure him. Streaks of blissful fire rushed through his veins, and his hips gave a few little bucks off the table before he spilled his own pleasure down Sigmund's throat.

The little man swallowed easily around him, his breath warm on Snow's skin, before he slowly drew back, giving the head of Snow's cock a few extra strokes with his tongue to not miss a drop, which made Snow jump and whine at the stimulation. Sigmund pulled away, and cool air brushed over his heated skin. He opened his eyes fully to see that Grim was completely ignoring them, urging the fire in the hearth back to life as if he were alone in the room.

Sigmund grinned, and Snow wrapped his arms around his neck, stroking his hair. "Thank you."

Sigmund laughed, leaning up to kiss him again. "Thank *you*, darlin'. Great way to start off my day."

Snow laughed as Sigmund helped him down from the table, and he slid his breeches back on.

"Heigh-ho, it's off to hunt I go," said Sigmund with a playful little hop in his step as he headed toward the door, grabbing the bow and arrows next to it.

Snow followed after him. "I wish you all the luck in the world, even if it makes me sad that you have to kill animals for food."

"You have such a good heart, Snow," Sigmund said, giving him a hug around the waist. Snow returned it, leaning down to give him another kiss. And then the little man was out the door into the slowly breaking dawn.

Snow glanced over at Grimwald, hearing stirring in the next room as the other little men seemed to be awakening. "I'm sorry you walked in on that first thing in the morning, Grim," he said with a small, apologetic smile.

Grim snorted. "I've woken up to much worse, kid. Trust me."

"I do," Snow said with a sweet smile and was delighted to see the faintest hint of a blush cross Grim's stoic features.

Fourteen

The next day, Dagobert was the one to stay home. Snow realized it had only been a week since he had come to this little cottage, but it already felt like he had been there for years. He was comfortable and happy, with seven men who cared about him, even loved him. All of the affection and friendship he had longed for as a child was being lavished upon him in spades by the little men who gave him kisses and praise and wanted to hear his stories of palace life.

The day was unnaturally warm for autumn, so Snow decided that working in the garden would be a good option. He wanted to clear away the weeds and clean up some of the vegetable rows, as well as pick all of the vegetables that were still there, for they would need them for winter.

Once the others had left, Dagobert joined him in cleaning up the breakfast dishes. Snow told him of the plan to work in the garden, and Dagobert beamed with happiness. "Do you want to help me?" Snow asked. The man nodded eagerly. "You don't have to hunt?"

Dagobert shook his head. Sigmund had had quite a bit of luck yesterday, finding several hares and wild turkeys, so they had meat both to eat now and to store for winter down in the root cellar on the other side of the house. Snow was happy that, despite the famine ravaging the land, the little men were doing all right preparing for the cold months ahead, when food would be even more scarce.

So, they spent the day in the garden. Snow had never tended a garden before, only received vegetables and herbs after they had been brought to the palace kitchens, and he spent several fascinated hours just looking at the different types of plants and how they grew.

"If we clear out the weeds, it should help for next year to create better soil where the good things grow," Snow said. He wasn't entirely sure what was weed and what was plant, but Dagobert seemed to, pointing out patches for him to pull out by hand or to dig out with a trowel. Snow wondered to himself as he dug his hands into the cool earth if he would still be here with the little men next spring when it came time for the plants to come to life once more. He had said he would only stay through the winter, but that was before he had spent time in their beds and getting to know each of them. Now the thought of leaving made his heart heavy. He thought that he might be able to be truly happy here with the seven little men that he cared about so much. Of course, it pained him that they were forced to dig in the dark mountains for gemstones that disappeared into the palace for his mother's magic use, for he knew that mining was a dangerous job. Several of the men had mentioned that they had lost friends and family along the way from it. But the spring was also far away, with braving the incoming winter the bigger priority. He dug his hands into the dirt again to scoop out the roots of a wild weed.

Next to him, Dagobert watched in fascination as the dirt disappeared from Snow's shirt as if it were never there. "My mother enchanted my clothing," Snow explained, flushing a bit. "So I would always look clean and proper, like a prince should. I embarrassed her in front of some important people, and she couldn't have that happen again."

Dagobert grinned and then pulled a stern, haughty look down his nose that reminded Snow so much of his mother that he burst into a fit of giggles. Dagobert joined him, the laughter overtaking them both until they were gasping for breath, and they ended up lying side by side on a bed of weeds and dirt in the garden.

"Sigurd told me you were only six years old when you were taken away from your family," Snow said softly once their laughter had subsided and they were silently lying next to one another.

Dagobert nodded.

"Do you remember much about your family?"

Dagobert slowly shook his head. He looked at Snow and made a circle gesture to the area around them. "The others are your family now?" Snow guessed, and Dagobert nodded, smiling a little now. "I suppose the mines then are all you have ever known."

Dagobert nodded again and gave a small shudder. Snow reached out and took the red-haired man's hand in his own. "I'm so sorry. I can't imagine what that must be like for you."

Dagobert smiled sadly at him and squeezed his hand.

"What would you do if you could do anything?" Snow asked curiously.

Dagobert's deep blue eyes blinked in surprise, and he looked very thoughtful. After a moment, he opened his mouth. "A writer," he said in his soft, mellow voice.

"Oh!" Snow breathed. "Have you written anything before?"

Dagobert's cheeks went pink, and he shook his head. "Never had time."

"Ah," Snow said, remembering that their life was indeed nearly entire subsistence. "Would you write something for me one day?"

Dagobert's eyes lit up, and he smiled brightly, nodding his head. Snow beamed back. "I can't wait."

Dagobert wrapped his arms around Snow's waist and tilted his head upwards hopefully. Snow held him close and leaned his own head down to press their lips together. Dagobert's mouth was warm and soft. Around them, the earthy scent of the plants and dirt reassured Snow that he was where he was supposed to be.

They ended up falling asleep in the garden like that, side by side and hand in hand, napping for several hours. Dagobert woke first. Upon opening his eyes, he discovered that two rabbits, a chipmunk, and a bluebird had come into the garden and were also curled up sleeping against Snow's sides and on his chest. He gazed lovingly at them, the dull sunlight shining down on the most beautiful man in the kingdom, who must have had a heart of pure gold for even the animals of the forest to love him as they did.

Snow stirred, and the animals did as well. When he opened his eyes and sat up, the animals all scattered, making Dagobert laugh out loud. Snow didn't think he had ever heard a sound more beautiful.

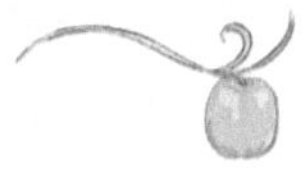

That evening, the little men returned to the cottage with interesting news they had gleaned from the guards as various people from further inland came to the mines with deliveries or to pick up the mined gemstones. It seemed that the Queen's Shadow had set fire to the castle and then disappeared. The throne room was in shambles. No one had been killed though, which Makellos was thankful for. He wondered what had caused the terrifying specter to not only turn on his mother, but have the ability to do so in the first place. Whatever it was, he suspected that was the reason he was still alive after the vicious attack a few days ago, and he was grateful for it. A charred throne room was a small price to pay for his life.

The next day, Der showed him how he would grind herbs and plants to make various tinctures, medicines, and remedies. Snow helped him fill several boxes with jars and bottles that would be taken to the market the following day to trade for things they needed.

"May I ask about you and Hardwic?" he asked as they worked on labeling the bottles with neat handwriting.

"Yes, of course," Der said, peering over the top of his spectacles at the bottle he held.

"How long have you two been together?"

"Well... I suppose it has been close to twelve years now," Der said thoughtfully. "I los- oh, this is very sad, are you certain you wish to hear it?"

"Yes," Snow said softly. "I want to know all about all of you and what happened. But only if you wish to tell it."

"Well, when we were brought here, I met another man. Ferdinand. He and I got along well together, and, when it became obvious that we were not escaping back to our old life, he and I..." Der waved his hand.

"Became lovers?" Snow ventured.

"Yes, I suppose that is the best way to put it. But, unfortunately, a few years later, he died. A mining accident." Der's voice had grown soft and distant. "We lost several friends that day."

"I'm so sorry," Snow whispered. "And yet you have to return each day to the same mine?"

"Yes," Der said, taking off his spectacles and digging out his ragged handkerchief to wipe them.

"I can't even imagine," Snow said softly. "Every one of you is so brave."

"Well, we don't have much choice," Der said with a sigh. "But we do what we can to be happy out here."

"Hardwic makes you happy?"

"Oh yes."

"But, you do not mind him being with... with me?" Snow asked.

"Oh, goodness, not at all," Der said, giving Snow a sunny smile. "One thing we have learned is that sharing everything and working together is the easiest way to survive. There are so many forms of love, and none are right or wrong. I always say, your heart never runs out of space. It just grows bigger to take it all in."

"I like that," Snow said with a soft laugh. "I have space for all of you in my heart too."

"As do we for you, my boy," Der replied, giving him a fond smile.

"I asked Bernhardt, but he said that Hardwic never talks about what he used to do before he came here."

"Oh, yes," Der said, clearing his throat a little nervously. "I... I actually do know, he... confided in me years ago. But I have sworn not to tell anyone. It is not my story to tell."

"Then you should say no more," Snow said, giving a solemn nod. He was not about to try to break the trust that Hardwic had put in his lover. Instead, he leaned down to give Der a quick kiss on the nose, because he knew it would make the older man blush, and it did.

There was a sudden knock at the wooden door of the cottage. Snow jumped. He had never heard that sound here, and certainly if the others had returned, they would just enter, not knock on their own door. Der looked surprised too, but not as much as Snow. "Go hide in the bedroom. I will see who it is," he said.

Snow hurried into the other room, moving to one corner to be as out of sight as possible, his heart racing. Could it be someone coming for him? Was Der about to be hurt because of him?

He could hear Der and another voice at the door talking for a few minutes before there was silence again, and Der came into the bedroom. "It's all right, you can come out now. A traveling lacemaker," he explained. "We do occasionally get peddlers who come by. It's not often, but the guards at the mine are always ready to spend coin on any amusement they can get to relieve their boredom."

"I'd believe that," Snow said with a soft chuckle, his heart finally slowing to its normal rhythm in his chest now that the possible danger had passed. "I imagine they have less to worry about when the palace takes care of all of their basic needs."

"Right you are, my boy. Status and money let people live very different lives, even if we all have the same amount of time."

Snow nodded slowly as they made their way back to the table where they had been working. "I've noticed. My days in the palace were much different than here. But," he added, giving Der a sweet smile, "I wouldn't give these up for anything."

"We love having you here with us, Snow. Though of course, we'd much rather you be safe and not have to hide at all."

"I just want to be able to help," Snow sighed. "There is so much change that needs to happen. I certainly could not do it all on my own. But under my mother, it will never happen."

"We can't predict what the future holds," Der said, giving his arm a light squeeze. "One day, everything might change. You never know."

Fifteen

Everything had fallen apart in a matter of days. Red had disappeared in the Dark Forest. Her son was still alive. Her geist had broken free from her control and torched a good chunk of the palace. The Queen's rage knew no bounds. For days, she locked herself in her chamber and would not open the door for anyone. But the servants could hear screams and the sound of breaking glass quite frequently. No one dared go near her. Nearly all of her meals remained untouched outside her door. Only her gemstones and other items she used in making her magical potions were accepted, the door opening quickly before being slammed once more with a thunderous crash.

Her huntsman had been a weak-willed man, his heart too feeble for such an important job. Her geist would have finished the task but for the magic that bound him to her being broken, and she could not recall him to her service, no matter how many spells she tried. It seemed that she was now on her own. Never send a man to do a woman's job, she thought to herself, especially one that you want done right. She would go herself and kill Makellos with her own hands. Then she would know the job was complete and done to her satisfaction. No frail shreds of sympathy, no unlucky ties being broken.

Once her mind was made up on this matter, she searched and searched through her books for weeks on end. She had to find the most appropriate and effective way to bring about Makellos' demise. Something simple. Brute force had not worked, nor had stealthy silence. It was time to try a more tender approach. Perhaps the only time she had ever considered being tender to her son, the radiant boy that had grown to outshine her. She needed something that would be easy to transport and that would hold its magic until it was called upon, for she would have to travel and search for him. Her Shadow had only told her the mountain foothills, and that spanned quite a long part in the south of the kingdom.

She finally found a manner that would be simple and effective. A poisoned brew that would bring about the Sleeping Death. It could be administered in a multitude of ways, but she already knew exactly how she could do it. Makellos loved apples. He always had, ever since he was a child. The beautiful ruby red ones were his favorite; he could never resist them. It was perfect. She would poison an apple, then travel the mountain range until she found where Makellos had hidden himself.

She read down the page to where the antidote was written. Every magical spell or potion could be reversed in some way, so she had to ensure that it was not a simple process to bring him back. Very few people, if any, would know the remedy for a black magic spell such as this, but there was certainly a chance at pure luck. At the bottom of the page, she read aloud to herself. "The victim of the Sleeping Death spell may be revived by True Love's Kiss."

She laughed a horrid laugh. No fear of that. She knew there was no one in the palace that he considered a True Love. She had seen to that throughout his childhood, that he never got too close to any of the servants, never spent a long time with any foreign nobles. Any love that he might have had in the palace would be unrequited; no one in the palace knew where the prince was anyway. And with luck, Makellos might be entirely alone in his hiding place. Even if he was not, surely whomever found him dead-asleep would bury him, or, better still, burn him upon a pyre. Once his eyes closed forever, she need not concern herself with what happened to his body.

She spent a sleepless night mixing the exact potion needed for the Sleeping Death. She summoned a servant to bring her a basket of fruit along with the most beautiful red apple in their storeroom. When the servant returned, the Queen took the single red apple into her hidden chamber where she had the bubbling concoction ready.

She dipped the apple into the swirling mixture. The sickly, viscous fluid clung to it like a coating of sugar. It seeped into the apple's tender skin like sand absorbing water, the apple shriveling like a shrunken head, turning black with withered pits like empty eye sockets in an ancient skull. Then it turned completely red once more, rosy bright. The perfect temptation.

She would need a disguise, for she could not go in her true form. The irony of shedding her beauty to track down Makellos was not lost on her. But it would be only temporary, and once Makellos was dead, she would never have to worry about him again. She found a spell to transform her queenly raiment and astonishing beauty into the guise of an ugly old peddler woman. She took the crushed gemstones and other elements needed, blending them together into a potion that she swallowed with no consternation. The world began to spin, and she collapsed to the floor of her chamber.

Her limbs twisted and became gnarled, like branches on a lifeless tree. Her golden hair turned a dull silver. Her butter soft skin with her rosy cheeks, ruby lips, and shapely eyes sunk and distorted, the hollows within them making her unrecognizable. Her elegant gown shriveled and darkened into muddy brown and midnight black, her shoes aging into patched and worn buckskin that barely covered her liver-spotted feet.

She rose to her feet and looked into her magic mirror. The face that looked back at her was hideous, twisted, and asymmetrical. Her stooped waist and hunched back gave her the appearance of an old, feeble woman. She shuddered, for she had never been more hideous in her life. But it was the perfect disguise to entrap the kind-hearted prince.

She placed the poisoned apple into the basket of fruit before she slipped out of the palace via one of the servant stairwells. She took one of the horses from the stable and rode it off into the darkness toward the south. The foothills would take time to search, and she did not wish to be slowed by guards or alert others to her presence. She would travel for days, weeks, months, for as long as it took until she found him. And when she did, she would complete the job the others had failed to do. Makellos, the fairest of all, would not live to see the next sunrise.

Sixteen

Snow had a plan. One he was more than a little excited about, if he was being honest with himself. In the almost two months he had been with the miners, he had shared their beds many times, often sweet and loving. But tonight, he was going to surprise them all. Well, all except Bernhardt, whose turn it was to stay home. He was going to need a little help, and there was no good way to ask the man to leave the cottage. This was something he wanted to do before the snow fell and it got too cold to really enjoy the idea. So, he explained the plan to Bernhardt, who eagerly accepted and even added a few thoughts of his own. Snow had forgotten that Bernhardt used to be an actor, so he had a flair for the dramatic and an eye for visual presentation.

As the sun descended low, Snow and Bernhardt prepared the evening surprise together. When everything was in place, Bernhardt agreed to wait outside for the others, and he sat out in the crisp evening of the woods, sipping a hot cup of tea and puffing on his pipe.

The other six miners returned a short while later to find the door and windows to the cottage closed and Bernhardt sitting on an overturned bucket by the door. "Is everything all right?" Der asked worriedly.

"Oh yes," Bernhardt said with a slightly mischievous smile. "Quite all right. Snow has a surprise for us all for dinner." There were murmurs of speculation, but finally everyone set aside their tools to go inside.

The cottage was warm and cheerful as always, lanterns lit and fire blazing in the hearth, and the delicious scent of roasted venison reached their noses. But the thing that caught every eye was the wooden dining table, upon which was placed their usual dishes and silverware. But in the center of the table lay Snow, without a stitch of clothing on. He lay on his back, resting peacefully. Upon his naked stomach was a platter of roasted meat. A bowl of colorful vegetables sat between his slightly spread legs. His skin gleamed in the lantern light, an almost golden hue. His dark head rested lightly on a single pillow on the table that tipped his head up just a bit so he could look down himself to the seven men in the doorway. "Welcome home," he said, his voice still sweet but dropped down into a more seductive purr. "Please, enjoy dinner."

Several of the little men just stood and stared. A few let out whistles and cheers, and Dagobert sprinted over to the table, nearly crashing into the bench in his haste to press his lips to Snow's in an enthusiastic kiss.

Snow smiled, having to hold still so the platter on his stomach did not go flying, but he kissed Dagobert back lovingly, moaning softly as he felt hands brush up over his bare feet and legs. He heard the scrape of the benches as the miners settled into their places around him. "Mmm, I ain't the prayin' type, but I thank whatever deities might be out there for this meal we are about to eat," Grim said, which produced guffaws of laughter from the others.

Snow had been worried that the little men would perhaps decide not to eat the meal he had prepared, so he was glad when each of them served up a piece of roasted venison and a spoonful of honey-slathered vegetables. A few droplets of the sauce fell onto his skin as the meal was dished out, sliding down his skin and tickling him, but someone would lean over and lick it up with their tongue, making him moan and squirm. His own cock had been half-hard to start, and each brush of lips or tongue over him, every reach across him, whether it touched him or not, sent a little thrill through him.

Dagobert lifted a forkful of meat and offered it to Snow's lips. Snow moaned and wrapped his mouth around it, chewing and carefully swallowing, his eyes locked with Dagobert's. The young man grinned at him. "Good?" he asked softly, so only Snow could hear.

Snow nodded. "Good," he agreed.

There were appreciative sounds all around as the little men ate the delicious meat and vegetables, each occasionally offering a bite to Snow's lips as well. Snow had gone all out with the meal he had prepared; honey sauce for the roasted vegetables, the meat perfectly cooked and seasoned, and fresh berries with whipped cream at the end. It was a delightfully delicious meal. Sigurd picked up a fat blackberry and pressed it to Snow's lips. The prince sighed in delight and opened his mouth, sucking the fruit in, his tongue brushing over Sigurd's fingers playfully as he did.

He almost leaped out of his skin as Bernhardt lifted a spoonful of the whipped cream and let it fall right onto Snow's erect cock. It slid down, sticky and sweet. "Oops," Berhardt said with a grin before he stood up on the bench and leaned down to lick his way over Snow's cock, clearing away the cream there. Rivulets of it melted and slid down past his balls, between his legs, and down into the crack between his cheeks. He knew it was just whipped cream, but the sticky, warm slide of it still made his cock throb and his hole ache eagerly.

"Well, I am ready for dessert," said Hardwic with a sweet smile. There was agreement all around as plates were rushed off the table, leaving Snow stretched out upon it as the only delicacy left.

"Mmm, thank you for the wonderful meal," Sigurd said, leaning down to press a kiss to Snow's lips. "Did you get enough to eat?"

Snow batted his lashes. "I am still very hungry," he said, hoping it sounded as seductive as he wanted it to be. It must have worked, because several of the men were already disrobing.

"Which of us do you want to eat?" Sigmund asked, already down to just his breeches and boots, which he was making fast work of.

"I want all of you," Snow said, narrowing his eyes. "I want to pleasure all of you together."

"Our insatiable little prince," teased Sigurd, and Snow giggled softly.

Grim moved behind his head. "Mm, back up, baby boy," he said. Snow shivered, sliding himself carefully back on the table so his head hung off the end of it. The blood that was not rushing to his cock rushed to his face, but he obediently opened his mouth when Grim's cock tapped against his cheek. Grim slid forward, and Snow whimpered, letting his throat loosen for Grim to slide all the way forward. He realized that this way he couldn't see what was happening on the table to the rest of him, but that was all right. As long as he pleasured his lovers, he was happy to do whatever they wanted. Tonight, he wanted to be used for their pleasure.

Sigmund wrapped his lips around Snow's cock, playing with the head with his tongue as Dagobert slid up between Snow's spread knees. The container of oil was already on the table, and he liberally slicked up his fingers before sliding one into Snow's hole. Snow moaned around the dick, his hips bucking eagerly toward Sigmund's mouth and Dagobert's fingers. He had stretched and oiled himself earlier too, which Dagobert seemed to realize, because he was able to add a second finger easily, making Snow whine pleadingly. Grim pressed his hips forward deeper into Snow's throat so he couldn't even make those noises.

Someone knelt up on the bench next to them, and Snow reached for the cock there, beginning to stroke it, slowly up and down, fondling the balls there. Sigmund's mouth on his cock licked and swirled around, teasing in a way that made his balls ache with need. He took a deep breath through his nose as the head of Dagobert's cock pressed to his hole and slowly slid in, the redhead letting out a gasp of desire. Another cock slid into his other hand, and he began to stroke that too. He heard a groan and turned his eyes slightly, seeing what he thought was Der and Hardwic nearby, groping and kissing, and his heart gave a little flutter. While he wanted to give all of his lovers pleasure tonight, he was very happy that they did not only feel the need to turn to him for affection and that perhaps some old sparks could reignite.

Dagobert only kept the thrusts slow and easy for a short time before he began to thrust hard and fast, deep into Snow. The prince's eyes watered at the pleasure pain, redoubling his efforts on Grim's cock, his hips bucking up toward Sigmund's mouth and Dagobert's thrusts, moaning and making soft pleading whimpers as the pleasure assailed him. With a gasp, Grim grabbed his shoulders and came down his throat. Snow did his best to swallow in his current position, but some of it dribbled out of mouth and down, or rather up, his cheek. Grim caught it with his thumb, brushing it down to Snow's mouth, and he eagerly sucked on it, giving the thumb pad a little nip as he did. Grim stroked his hair, leaning down to kiss him. "Good boy."

Snow whimpered pleadingly, and one of the cocks in his hand, which he realized was Sigurd, moved to replace Grim at the head of the table and slid his cock into Snow's throat. He took it down with a pleading noise, little cries escaping him as Sigmund and Dagobert made his head spin with pleasure. His back arched as Dagobert thrust hard into him and spilled himself, grinding his hips against Snow's as his hips pumped and his cock throbbed and pulsed. His own cock ached for release, but Sigmund's mouth on him was so delicate and light that he knew it would take him forever to come that way, which he was sure was the point. He had learned over the many weeks that, for as much of a flirt as Sigmund was, he was also an incredible cocktease.

Dagobert slid out of him, pressing kisses down Snow's thighs and legs before he stepped away. Snow's empty hole pulsed pleadingly. The cock in his hand moved away as Bernhardt crawled onto the table. He slid between Snow's spread knees. He already had the container of oil in his hands and his fingers coated with it. He slid two fingers inside of Snow, who moaned and grunted softly, spreading his legs wider as he swallowed around Sigurd.

There were kisses and touches all over his legs and torso as the others gathered around, and he reached out to stroke his fingers over faces and hair, whatever he could reach in his tipped back position.

Bernhardt's fingers were not very long or thick, but he knew how to use them inside of Snow's quivering passage.

Sigmund pulled back from Snow's cock with a soft pop, leaving him wet and aching. He cried out in frustration around Sigurd's cock, trying to focus instead on Bernhardt's fingers. Bernhardt slid two more fingers inside of him, so four of his small digits were sunk into Snow's ass, stretching him wider. He moaned, then let out a gasping cry around the dick in his mouth as someone's tongue brushed over the soft skin between his balls and where Bernhardt's fingers were buried inside of him. The little fingers flexed, his ass quivering a little. He felt more lube slide into him via Bernhardt's fingers, and then something else probed his ass, he thought it was a thumb. He took a deep breath through his nose as he sucked upside-down on the dick as the thumb popped inside of him, fingers pinched together to make it all a little smaller, and he felt Bernhardt's slender hand slide deep inside of him, up to what felt like his wrist. He let out a pleading squeal, and the dick in his mouth was removed so he could talk. "Too much?" asked Bernhardt.

"No," Snow said breathily. "No, it... it's wonderful..." He tried to lift his head, but he was so distracted by the pleasure-pain stretch of Bernhardt's hand and the pressure building in his head, that he couldn't make his neck work.

"Here, roll over," someone said, maybe Der. Hands shifted on him, and he allowed them to guide him. Bernhardt's full hand stayed buried inside of him as multiple other hands helped Snow to sit up and roll over onto his stomach, letting out a pleading groan as his ass rotated around Bernhardt's fist. He pushed himself up onto his hands and knees, bowing his head low as Bernhardt's angle changed inside of him, and he let out a soft cry.

"Yes! Fuck!"

A dick appeared in front of him, and he opened his mouth to take it in as Bernhardt's full hand pressed in and out of him, smaller than the average person's hand but still stretching him open wide. Out of the corner of his eye, he saw one of the men, he couldn't quite see who, kneel on the bench next to him and present their cock. His mouth was engaged, so he took it in his hands, stroking lovingly over it, up and down, squeezing the balls and back up again, starting up a rhythm to match his mouth's movements, his hips pushing back into Bernhardt's fist. Even without stimulation now, his cock was hard and throbbing, and he wanted to come so badly already, but he wanted this to last as long as it could.

"Mmm, do you think you could take me and someone else at the same time?" Bernhardt asked as his hand slid in and out of Snow's ass, slick with the oil.

Snow knew that Bernhardt's cock was in proportion to the rest of him, so it was not overly large. His cheeks went pink as he eagerly stroked the dick in his hand that he realized was Sigmund, taking Der's cock out of his mouth to reply, "I would like to try."

"Mm, let's do this on the bed," said Der logically. "We don't need anyone falling off the table."

"Spoilsport," muttered Sigmund.

And then the hands were all gone from him, leaving him cold and empty and breathless. Snow lifted his head, whimpering softly at the loss of sensation and his cock still bobbing heavy between his legs. Hands were offered to him to help him down off the table, and he slowly did, realizing how sticky he already was. His feet wobbled, and several pairs of hands steadied him. He wasn't even completely sure he could walk straight with his ass aching to be filled and his cock straining for release, but the hands on him stayed firm. They made their way to the bedroom.

"Mmm, kneel right there," Hardwic said, pointing to the edge of the bed. Snow did as he was told, dropping to his knees and bending his torso over the bed, sticking out his ass behind him.

"I need more," he begged softly.

"Oh, you'll get it," said Sigmund, crawling onto the bed before turning his back to Snow and bending down, pressing his hips back. Snow didn't even think, just leaned in and ran his tongue over Sigmund's tight asshole, stroking and rubbing with the tip of his tongue. Someone knelt beside him and began to stroke his aching cock with rough, calloused hands. He thought it might be Grim, but right now, he couldn't be sure of anything. The world felt warm and slippery, and all that mattered was the heat and the touches and the growing need inside of him.

Bernhardt ran his hand down Snow's back. "Ready, beautiful?"

"Mm-hmm," Snow murmured as his tongue continued to flicker and press over Sigmund's hole. He heard the sound of slick hands stroking over cocks, and then Bernhardt pressed inside of him. It was not as thick as his hand, and Snow let out a breath, trying to relax. The hand on his cock gave him a warm squeeze, and he whined, soft and needy. And then the hand was gone, and someone was sliding underneath him, guiding his hips downward. Another cock head pressed to his hole, this one much wider. He was pretty sure it was Hardwic. He gasped, his hands catching the edge of the bed as he braced himself. "Breathe, baby boy," said Der in his ear. Snow did as he was told, taking a deep breath and letting it out. The second cock head popped inside of him, and he let out a cry as the two cocks stretched him to an almost eye-watering width. "All right?" asked

Der, and Snow nodded eagerly, taking another deep breath before turning his attention back to Sigmund.

Hardwic and Bernhardt rocked back and forth with him, Hardwic thrusting up, Bernhardt rolling his hips forward so they were moving in and out of Snow at the same time. He panted softly at the fullness pressing into him, continuing to swirl his tongue around Sigmund's asshole before he was nudged aside, and Der's cock pressed to his lips. He opened his mouth to take it in, swirling his tongue around the head before closing his lips to suck on him. Another cock slapped playfully at his cheek, and he reached up to stroke it. He opened his eyes, not sure when he had closed them, to see Sigurd next to Der. Beyond them, he could see three others on the bed. He realized with a little flutter of delight that Dagobert was bouncing up and down on Grim's cock as he sucked eagerly on Sigmund's.

Hardwic and Bernhardt were speeding up their thrusts now, and Snow savored the ache of it inside of him, his eyes rolling a little as he put extra effort into sucking on Der and stroking Sigurd. He wasn't sure how much time had passed, but it felt like both forever and nothing as Bernhardt came first inside of him, and Hardwic followed a few moments later, grinding against Makellos, and he whimpered, needy and tearful.

When Hardwic and Bernhardt pulled out, he felt a cold, empty ache deep inside of him, and he moved his mouth away from Der just long enough to beg, "Please, more."

Sigurd gave him a sweet kiss before he moved around behind him, and Makellos heard him slick over himself with the oil. He took Der back into his mouth, sucking on the head of his prick until Sigurd slid deep inside of him, pushing him forward, using that to take

Der deeper into his mouth again. Der let out a string of words that were probably meant to be curses but really were nothing more than nonsense, his hands sliding into Snow's hair to hold and stroke him. Snow moaned, then let out a yelp around the cock as someone, he suspected Hardwic, sealed their mouth around his own dripping cock and began to suck.

The pleasure he had been holding back caught up with him when his balls were squeezed as the hot throat swallowed around his shaft, and Snow stilled, his back arching, as he let out a wail of pleasure around Der's cock as Sigurd continued to thrust in and out of him, finding the spot inside of him that made him see stars. It felt like his orgasm stretched on endlessly, and he momentarily forgot to breathe, reminded when Der's cock gave a little jump in his mouth, and he gasped, tears running down his cheeks as he continued to suck on him.

"Such a good boy, Snow," Der panted, his hands stroking through Snow's midnight-dark hair. "Such a good boy for his Daddies."

The praise made him feel warm all over and caused a few happy tears to flow down his cheeks. He wanted to be a good boy for his lovers, the men who had all been so kind and loving to him.

Sigurd let out a howl of pleasure as he pulled out and shot his load across Snow's sleek back and ass cheeks. Snow whined, his hole pulsing and pleading for more. Sigmund had left Grim and Dagobert to finish what they were doing, and he stretched out now on the bed on his back. "Want to ride this dick until you can't see straight, beautiful?" he asked Snow.

"Yes," Snow pleaded, looking up at Der. "And you."

Der laughed and stroked his cheek. "Hungry little princeling. Get up on the bed."

"Yes, Daddy," Snow whimpered, crawling up onto the bed where Sigmund was stroking himself with oil. Snow crawled over him to kiss him, feeling sticky all over but still wanting, *needing* more. It was all he wanted right now, all he ever wanted. To be loved and cared for, and to love in return. He shifted to straddle Sigmund's hips and slid down his shaft with a gasp of pleasure, his back arching as he comfortably seated himself. He started to rock his hips, trying to find a rhythm and angle he liked, when he felt Der press up behind him. He paused his movements until the older man's cock pressed against his already tightly-stretched hole. Snow tensed for a moment, knowing this was going to hurt to start, but Hardwic stepped up in front of him, standing over Sigmund, offering his thick cock to Snow's lips. Snow opened his mouth obediently, and Hardwic slid down his throat, slowly, stroking his hair, as Der's cock head pressed hard against him and then popped inside. Snow let out a yowl like a cat in heat around Hardwic's cock as the second cock stretched him wider than he had ever been before, whining as his hips gave a little buck downward toward Sigmund's cock. "Just like that," Der soothed as he slid forward, stroking over the prince's lower back with his hands. "Such a good boy, Snow."

The words made Snow flush all over, his insides tensing and quivering. He sucked eagerly on Hardwic's cock that stretched open his lips with its girth, letting Sigmund and Der set the pace beneath him with their thrusts. He felt so full, running his hand down his lower stomach to feel them inside of him.

Bernhardt and Sigurd climbed up on either side of him, their cocks erect and dripping. Makellos began to stroke both of them, one with each hand, as he sucked and swallowed and teased Hardwic's with his tongue. His body pumped up and down on Der and Sigmund's cocks. They suddenly stopped thrusting, and Snow released Hardwic's cock for a moment to turn and look over his shoulder.

Dagobert and Grim had come to join them all. Grim had slicked up his cock and his hand and was currently sliding his fingers in and out of Der, the old apothecary moaning and arching his back into Grim's touch. Snow's heart gave a little delighted jump, turning back to Hardwic. Past him, Dagobert was straddling Sigmund's shoulders, and the brown-haired man was eagerly sucking on his cock while Snow rode him. Snow moaned and went back to bobbing his head on Hardwic's shaft. He felt when Grim pushed himself inside Der, the weight pushing Der deep into him, and he let out another pleading squeal of pleasure.

They were all together now, each of them attached to the group, and Snow had never felt so loved or so needed. He felt wanton, nearly crazed by lust, as his own cock bounced eagerly in time with Der and Sigmund's thrusts. His hands stroked Bernhardt and Sigurd as he leaned back against Der, his eyes hazy as he sucked on Hardwic. If he could just stop time and feel this forever, he knew he would always be happy.

"Gonna... come..." Hardwic warned, his small hands tangling in Snow's hair. Snow moaned in encouragement, and, a moment later, his mouth was full of Hardwic's release. He sucked at the head and swallowed it down as best he could. Hardwic drew away with a soft groan, pressing a kiss to his lips, his tongue sweeping into Snow's mouth to taste himself there. Snow tangled their tongues together, panting softly. When Hardwic pulled back, Snow turned his head to take Bernhardt into his mouth and suck on him as he squeezed and rolled his balls in his palm. He did that for several moments, then turned his head to switch to Sigurd on the other side, doing the same. He suddenly found another cock in front of his face, and he lifted his eyes to Dagobert in front of him. With an eager moan, he surged forward, Der helping to prop him up, taking Dagobert's leaking cock into his mouth and down his throat. He let the momentum of Der and Sigmund's thrusts deep into him pull him back and forth on Dagobert's cock, making soft grunting, whining noises as the pleasure assailed him.

He eagerly sucked down one cock, giving it a few swallows around his throat as his hands stroked two others, then switching to take another into his mouth and stroke over two more. He wasn't even sure whose was whose anymore; all he knew was that he wanted all of them, wanted to bring each of them as much pleasure as he could.

Dagobert grabbed his hair to pull him off of his cock as he began to come, his warm seed hitting Snow in the face, some of it in his open mouth, and he stretched out his tongue, eager to catch it. Something warm hit his cheek, and he realized that Bernhardt was coming too. Snow tipped his head back, sticky seed splattering over his eyes and forehead. He kept his eyes closed, making little panting and mewling sounds as Sigmund and Der's thrusts became harder and faster, letting his body go completely under their mercy as they fucked him. Someone wrapped their lips around his bobbing cock and sucked eagerly. The head of Sigurd's cock slid into his open mouth as he cried out, and he swallowed it down eagerly, his eyelashes and brows too sticky to open. He felt more seed splatter his face, his chest, his hair, down his throat, all of it warm and reminding him of how much he was loved. He swallowed the mouthful, then gave a scream as the mouth on his cock gave a powerful suck, and his orgasm rocked through him like he had been struck by lightning.

His body jerked and spasmed as his balls emptied themselves into the hot mouth, spilled seed dripping down his face, neck, and chest, pooling into the creases and crevices of his skin. His body still moved, ass pulsing in pleasure, and then Der was coming, and Sigmund too, grinding themselves against him in a way that made him see stars and brought a wild scream of rapture to his lips. He felt himself collapsing forward into a warm embrace, the world too bright, his body both too heavy and floating at the same time.

He wiped clumsily at the stickiness on his face, his chest rising and falling eagerly as he sank down against a pillow, heart fluttering, his body singing with sensation all over. His ass ached, his balls were tight, he was sticky and itchy all over from spent passions drying on his skin, in his hair, and inside of him. But he had never in his life felt more satiated or more loved. His seven lovers had each loved him in their own way, bathed him in their affection and desire, pleasured him and let him pleasure them in return, and he was sure he could never be happier than he was right now with all of them holding him and surrounding him with love.

He became aware of a wet cloth wiping gently at his face, first his eyes, then over his nose and mouth, clearing away the mess there until he was able to open his eyes without trouble again. Bernhardt had a cloth that he was using to wipe Snow's face tenderly. Someone spread his legs, and he looked down to see Dagobert wiping carefully between the globes of his ass. He knew he was probably going to be leaking seed all night, but he was perfectly all right with that. He wanted all of them to know that he belonged to them, that he loved each of them, that he would always be faithful and loyal to them, his seven little lovers.

Grimwald pressed a cup of fresh, cool water to his lips, and Snow obediently drank it down. The cloth cleaning his face moved on to his chest and torso, wiping away the sticky streaks left on his skin. Someone helped him roll over onto his side so that his back could be washed as well. When he was settled once more onto his back, his eyes were burning with the desire to sleep, and they drifted shut as a warm blanket was draped over him. "I love you all, each and every one of you," he whispered. Each of them echoed the sentiment back to him, but he didn't hear any of them because he was already fast asleep.

Seventeen

The Queen traveled alone up and down the lands close to the southern foothills. She encountered some travelers and villagers as she searched, but no one had knowledge of a young man with skin as pure as snow and hair as black as ebony. Every day that did not yield up Makellos' location fanned the wind of her hatred.

She had searched high and low without success when she heard tell of a small cottage in a clearing where the men who mined the hills lived. So, the next morning, she set out for the area near the mines, tying her horse to a tree and wandering on foot past a burbling stream until she smelled chimney smoke and saw golden thatch peeking through the trees. She followed the gleam to the edge of the tree line, and there she found a cottage, a humble dwelling with a garden and a well. She hid just out of sight behind the trees and watched the house intently. The little men had already left for work, it seemed, for the house was quiet.

The heavy front door opened, and a familiar figure stepped out. Makellos had a broom in his hand and swept over the threshold, whistling a jaunty tune as he did. The sound of it made her jaw clench. She had told him many times as a child that whistling was vulgar. Not that it mattered though, for he would be dead shortly. She started to step out of the trees, then quickly ducked back in.

Someone besides Makellos was at the house. She peered out from behind the tree again. A short man with chestnut hair and a pointed beard had appeared in the doorway, carrying a bow and arrow. He was quite diminutive. She vaguely recalled they were not far from the mines where she had sent the little men of the kingdom all those years ago. This must be one of them, she reasoned.

She watched as Makellos leaned down and pressed a kiss to the man's lips. The little man hugged him around the neck as he kissed him back before he set off into the woods. She shrank back behind the tree as he approached the tree line. She heard him walk across several crunchy leaves and twigs, close by, before the sound faded again, leaving the area in wooded silence once more. She stepped out from behind the tree. The door to the little cottage was closed now, but the window next to it stood open, at which she could see Makellos in his ever-white shirtsleeves, filling a bucket with water from a pump. She approached the little cottage, her back bent as if with age, clutching her basket tightly. "Fruit for sale," she called, her voice a haggard croak. "Lovely fresh fruit for sale."

Makellos looked out the window, his blue eyes meeting her own, and she gave him a small, toothless grin. "Hello, good sir," she said, lifting her bony hand in a wave. "Might I interest you in some fresh fruit today?"

The poor older woman looked to be no more than a whisp that would be blown away by the wind. And being able to offer his lovers a fresh fruit tart would be a wonderful surprise as well. Makellos opened the door and stepped out into the crisp air. "Good morning. I believe I would be interested. May I offer you a seat, ma'am?"

"So polite," she cooed. "Don't worry about an old woman's comfort, dear boy."

"Please, I insist," Makellos said, offering her his elbow. She took it and hobbled over the threshold into the little cottage, casting her eyes about for anyone else who might be in the way of her plans, but it seemed as if they were all alone.

Makellos sat her upon one of the wooden benches. "May I offer you tea or something else to drink?"

"Oh, no, no," the woman said, waving her hand dismissively. "I am more spry than you might think, dearie." Makellos laughed and sat on the bench next to her. "My, you are a strapping young lad, aren't you? What is your name?"

"The little men call me Snow White," he said, giving her a kind smile.

"Snow White." The Queen had to stop herself from cackling aloud. What a silly, childish name, for a silly, childish boy. Makellos looked none the worse for wear after his attempted assassinations. In fact, if anything, he looked even more fair. His blue eyes sparkled with delight, and his cheeks were pink and rosy. Her hatred boiled within her like molten lead, but she just gave him another smile as set her basket upon the table. The bright red apple was on the very top of the pile, the only apple in the lot. "The little men are not here?"

"No," Makellos said. "They work at the mines in the mountains. I tend the house for them."

"What a good boy you are," the Queen said, reaching up a withered hand to pat his cheek. "I am sure they would love some fresh fruit after a hard day's work."

"I am certain they would," Makellos said brightly. "Please let me see your wares."

The Queen pushed the basket toward him, and, sure enough, Makellos' eyes landed directly on the single bright red apple at the top. "Ah, you are a lover of apples, good sir?"

"Indeed, I am," Makellos said with a sheepish grin. "And it has been a long while since I have had a fresh one."

"Oh, poor lad," the Queen said. "I only have the one apple. Please, take it for yourself, no payment required."

"Oh, I couldn't do that!" Makellos said, his blue eyes wide. The idea of taking something for free from this poor old woman when he had the means to pay her with some of the silver squirreled away in the cottage did not sit right with him.

"Please," the Queen said, plucking the rosy fruit from the basket and holding it out to him with both hands. "I insist. Then you will know how sweet and fresh the rest of my wares are." She held out the bright red apple toward him.

Makellos took the apple from her hands. "You are so very kind," he said, giving her a warm smile. He lifted the fruit to his nose and gave it an inhale. The Queen's heart quickened, watching him closely. He sank his teeth into the apple with a satisfying crunch as he broke through the blood-red skin into the white flesh beneath it.

As he chewed the bite, his vision suddenly swam and melted before him, making the world into streaks of watercolor. His head pounded ferociously, and his limbs felt heavy, like they were dragging him to the ground. He took a breath that felt like nothing in his lungs. A coldness spread over him, starting at his lips and moving outward and downward. There was a thump as the apple fell from his hand onto the floor, his fingers no longer able to clench. As the cold seeped into his knees, his vision went white. He fell off the bench and collapsed to the floor in a sprawl of limbs. He let out one more breath that expelled everything in his lungs, and the whiteness in front of his eyes faded to nothing as they closed. Prince Makellos was dead.

The Queen cackled with laughter as she saw his stillness at her feet. "Foolish boy," she said. "Your heart was too tender, and I am once more the fairest in the land." She picked up her basket and left the cottage with a swish of her dark cloak. She hurried to where she had left her horse, and she set off back toward the castle once more, confident now that when she asked the mirror who was the fairest, there would be only one answer it could give.

Sigmund returned a time later, bearing the carcasses of several fat hares over his shoulder. The weather was suddenly icy cold, his breath visible in the air as he walked. Winter would be upon them very soon. The door to the cottage was closed, the house quiet. Perhaps Snow had laid down for a nap or was sitting by the fire darning socks. He opened the door, and his bow and the leash of hares hit the floor with a thump.

Snow was lying on the ground by one of the benches, limbs akimbo, his head tipped at an odd angle. Sigmund rushed forward, dropping to his knees next to him and giving him a shake. "Snow!" he said urgently. The body under his hands flopped listlessly. The blue eyes were closed, as if asleep, but the body was so heavy. Sigmund looked at his chest for signs of breath, but he saw no rise and fall there. He leaned down, pressing his ear to the young man's chest, but he heard no flutter of a heartbeat either. "No," he moaned, lifting the prince's head and peeling back one eyelid. The beautiful sky-blue eye was lifeless and staring. "No, no, no, no..." Sigmund rocked the prince gently in his arms. "Fuck, I shouldn't have left you," he murmured, tears making their way down his cheeks. "You can't be gone, beautiful, you can't. We love you so much. We love you. Please come back to us." He sat there on the floor, Makellos' head curled in his lap, rocking him gently and stroking his hair. And it was there that the six other miners found him when they returned at the end of the day.

"What happened?" Der asked in shock, dropping his tools and rushing forward. The others crowded behind him, and then there was screaming and commotion as they all surged inside and saw the horrific sight before them.

"I found him like this," Sigmund said, barely looking up. His cheeks were bright red from crying, his eyes so swollen that he was squinting up at Der.

"Let me see," Der said gently, but there was a catch in his voice as he knelt next to Sigmund. Sigurd stepped up behind his brother, placing his hands on the man's shoulders and squeezing lightly.

Der felt as if his heart was broken into a million pieces. Behind him, Dagobert was on his knees screaming, the sound muffled into Hardwic's chest as tears flowed down the round man's face and into his beard. Bernhardt was nearly hyperventilating, and Grim was just staring with the most blank look on his face that Der had ever seen. If Sigmund had found him in this state, it was far too late for any extraordinary measures. It didn't seem possible that their dear, sweet, kind-hearted prince, who loved animals and baking and had been so kind and passionate with all of them, was gone.

They needed some answers. Der pulled off his spectacles, wiping tears off of them with a cloth from his pocket and put them back on, but the tears had only streaked further. More of them made fresh tracks down his face as he carefully lifted Makellos into his arms.

Der checked his throat, but there was nothing lodged there; he had not choked to death, despite the apple with a single bite out of it that lay a short distance away. He checked him all over for bruises or signs of a struggle. But there was nothing at all.

"Had to be magic," Grim muttered, more to himself but loud enough for the others to hear. "He was fine this morning, fit as a fiddle." He pulled out a handkerchief from his pocket and gave his nose a great honk into it.

They washed his body and hair with soap in case he had been poisoned by something he touched, but there was no indication anywhere of why their beloved prince was dead on the floor. Tears streamed down every face, though Dagobert continued to sob the loudest, unable to even touch the prince without breaking out in heart-wrenching wails. They dressed him once more in his perfectly clean shirtsleeves, pants, and boots. And then came the question of what to do with him.

They had dealt with death before; many of their friends and family had died over the years in the mines, and most of them were laid to rest in the forest, buried when they were able. But it was dark outside now, the pain still a fresh wound. So, they placed him on their collective large bed and sat a vigil around him all night, the flickering lanternlight playing off of his pale skin, still so smooth and full even in death. The only sound all night was the occasional sniffle or clearing of the throat as each reflected on their dear prince who had left them far too soon.

Dawn came, and none of them stirred. The thought of going to work now, of plunging into the dark, musty mines, seemed like an impossible feat. It was long after they should have left for work when Bernhardt finally broke the heavy silence. "Is anyone hungry?"

They all were, for they had had no supper, but the thought of eating anything right now seemed like too great a task. Still, Bernhardt rose to his feet, and Hardwic followed him. Together, they set about putting together a simple meal of bread and cheese. All of them gathered around the table that suddenly seemed much too large and empty without Makellos' bright laughter and warm presence there. They ate with only a few mumbles in between, and then they all sat silent once more.

"Shall... shall we bury him?" ventured Der, his voice low and cautious, as if afraid to give voice to his thought.

That sent Dagobert into another wail of grief, and several others flinched. They knew they could not leave him as he was forever. But the thought of putting their beloved Makellos in the ground, amongst the dirt and worms, was too much for them bear with their sorrow still so overwhelming. "One more day," Hardwic said softly.

That elicited nods and mumbles around the table. One more day to sit with their thoughts and their heartache before they would do their best to try to move forward without the ray of sunshine that had come into their lives and changed them all for good.

Dagobert was still sobbing. Der stroked his back gently. "Here now, Dag, you should get some rest. Let's... let's bring the prince in here, so there is a place of privacy."

No one objected, nor did any of them protest when they carried Makellos in their arms once more into the living space and set him carefully on the table. They placed a blanket under him and changed the blankets on the bed as well. A few movements were made to return to normalcy. Dagobert was put to bed. Wise old Bernhardt took the blankets to wash and then hung them to dry in front of the fire that Sigurd stoked back to life. Dishes were cleaned, tools were sharpened, another meal was eaten. All of this happened in relative silence. The life that the beautiful prince had brought into the cottage was gone, leaving it cold and drab, a prison once more.

Occasionally, one or two of them would stop and sit on a bench and hold the prince's hands or press soft kisses to his cheeks and forehead. They spoke to him in soft voices, whispered secret words in his ear. Told him how much they loved him and what he had meant to them, with his kindness and creativity and loving spirit. His passion and his lack of favoritism as he made love to each of them in his own way.

As darkness settled over the woods once more, most of them headed off to bed, bringing Dagobert a plate of food as well that the young man picked silently at. Grimwald sat up, wrapped in a blanket, sitting on the bench next to Makellos, a cup of lukewarm tea clutched in his hands. "It ain't fair," he grumbled softly. "It ain't fair."

Eighteen

The oppression of dawn was heavy on all of them the next morning. There was again no talk of going to the mines. The priority today would be to bid a final farewell to their dear, sweet Snow White, the fairest in all the land. The sunlight through the windows was dull and gray like their thoughts as they gathered around the table.

"Does anyone wish to speak?" Der asked softly.

There was silence all around. Even Dagobert had finally ceased his wild sobs, too wrung out from crying to do more than lean on Hardwic's shoulder.

Sigmund finally spoke up. "I think we all know that we lost something very special. Something that we were lucky to ever find in the first place."

"He loved all of us, and we all loved him," said Sigurd, squeezing his brother's shoulder. "He was a diamond in the mine, the most beautiful of all."

"He had the most wonderful laugh," said Hardwic.

"And he could dance like an angel," Bernhardt added.

"Perfect," croaked Dagobert, to which everyone nodded their heads in silent agreement.

"Grim?" Der asked, giving the dark-eyed man a glance. "Would you like to say something?"

Grimwald opened his mouth, but nothing came out. He tried again, then fell silent, bowing his head as a tear tracked down his cheek. That tear was worth a thousand words.

"Let's say our final goodbyes," Der said, his voice breaking a little. "Then we can find a place for him to rest in the forest, with all of the animals he loved so much."

That prompted a few sad smiles, and the little miners gathered around the head of the table. Each stepped up and pressed a kiss to their beautiful lost prince, some upon the forehead, others upon the cheek or hands. The last one to step up was Dagobert. He bent down, tears burning once more upon his pink cheeks, about to bestow his kiss when a sudden racket outside startled them all.

Through the trees burst three guards on horseback. They could see them through the crack between the casement of their front windows that were currently shut. The guards from the mines. One, the head of the guards with a great purple plume on his helmet, hopped down from his horse and hurried to the wooden door of the cottage, banging upon it with his fist. "Open up in the name of Queen Schön of Falchovari!"

The little men looked about in panic, for they had the prince of Falchovari dead upon their dining table and the royal guard at the door. Grim was the first to react, grabbing Sigmund and Dagobert by the collars and yanking them toward the bedroom. Der watched them go before more pounding at the door again startled him. "One moment," he called, his voice high and shaky.

"Open this door immediately!" yelled the guard, battering his fist upon the door, enough that a few strands of loose thatch from the roof fell down upon their heads. "If you do not, we're coming in."

Grim came sprinting back into the room with a blanket, Sigmund and Dagobert at his heels with blankets of their own. Grim tossed the blanket over Makellos' head and shoulders, hitting Bernhardt in the face with the fabric as it sailed over the table. Sigmund draped the second blanket across Makellos' middle, and Dagobert across his legs. They had just finished covering him when the door burst open with a crack of splintering wood and the screech of hinges coming loose, the three guards all surging inside at once. They stopped short, the little men staring up at the guards, the guards staring in return at the shrouded figure upon the table.

Hardwic was the first to recover his senses. "Our apologies, gentlemen," he said, letting tears flow down his ruddy cheeks. "Our dear friend was taken ill and passed suddenly, and our grief has known no bounds."

The lead guard's thick moustache bristled, and he gave a stumbling little huff. "Be that as it may, you are still required to work."

Der glanced around at the others and gave a small nod. If the guards stood here much longer, they might investigate, and find that the missing prince was dead under the blankets. "Yes, we... we shall go."

"All of you," the lead guard said gruffly.

The little men looked amongst themselves with concern that no one would be left here to take care of Makellos. But the more they protested, the more suspicious the guards might become. "Yes. Let us bank the fire so it does not get too warm in here," Der said, nodding to Sigurd who was closest to the hearth. "We shall have to bury our friend upon our return."

"The ground is frozen," piped up one of the guards behind the lead one. He was younger and seemed at least a little remorseful at the situation. "Snow came last night." He stepped aside for the little men to see out the door, and, indeed, there was several inches of clean, white snow blanketing the ground.

The little men all glanced around one another again. They did not want to leave Makellos as he was, but if they were to try to move him, it was possible the blankets might slip and reveal his face. So, Sigurd banked the fire, casting the little cottage into dimness and cold. Then the little men all grabbed their warm clothing and queued up for the walk to the mines together. The last one out of the cottage was Grimwald, who propped the broken door shut as best he could.

Because they had missed the day before, the guards were not eager to release them when it became dark. It was rumored that the Queen had been in a terrific rage recently, and if their quota of jewels was lacking, she might wreak her vengeance on them. So, the seven little miners toiled longer hours until the black of night made it impossible to work further. But instead of going home, the guards had them sleep in the mine, with rocks for pillows and thin blankets as coverings, to begin work anew as soon as dawn peeked over the horizon.

Though they spoke not a word about him, they could see in one another's eyes the worry about Makellos being left alone in their cottage. They had been visited by death before, but the suddenness of its arrival on one so young and fair had shocked them all into stony silence. More than one of them broke down deep inside the mine, crying and even wailing, such that it might have been thought a banshee creature inhabited the thick darkness.

The ground was frozen now; they could not give him a proper burial. They decided quietly amongst themselves that once the spring came and the ground was thawed, they would lay him to rest properly under the forest floor, the way they had for many of their fallen friends and relatives. It was nightfall before they were allowed to return home once more, trudging through the heavy, wet snow toward their cottage that would feel empty and cold now without Makellos' sunshine to fill it.

They had just reached the clearing and saw their house when Der came to a sudden stop, causing several of them to crash into him, nearly taking them all to the slippery ground. "The light's lit!" he gasped.

And indeed, he was correct. Where they had left their home yesterday without lighted lantern or hearth, a warm, yellow glow now emanated from the windows and from under the sturdy wooden door that was no longer propped up but attached once more in proper working order.

They nearly all tripped over one another as they slipped and skidded across the clearing to the little cottage. Dagobert arrived at it first, but his hands were shaking so badly that he was unable to grab the wrought iron handle. Bernhardt reached past him and opened the latch of the door, swinging it inside with its usual high-pitched squeak.

All of the lanterns around the cottage burned brightly, and a large fire blazed in the hearth, filling the room with its warmth and light. Upon the wooden table, where they had left the prince wrapped in his hasty veil, the three blankets now sat, neatly folded, with a piece of parchment resting atop it. The body of the prince was nowhere to be seen.

All of them stood and stared for a very long time before Sigurd voiced what they were all thinking. "What in the Queen's cunt is going on?"

They all approached the table as though it were enchanted and might come to life, but it was their same table with its many gouges and scratches, the benches neatly tucked in under it. Der picked up the parchment, which was simply folded and sealed with a drop of wax bearing a sigil. "What is this?" He held the parchment up for all to see.

"The Thieves Guild," breathed Hardwic, to everyone's surprise. Sigurd and Sigmund turned to look at him suspiciously, but Hardwic just smiled and shrugged. "It's the same as the symbol on the carts that bring supplies to the mine."

Der broke the wax seal with slightly shaky fingers, squinting at the writing, then setting it down to wipe at his spectacles that were stained with melted snow. Grimwald let out an annoyed huff and snatched up the paper, glaring at the flowing script as he read aloud.

"To the seven little men of the mines.

Our deepest condolences for the loss of Prince Makellos. He is resting peacefully in your garden. But all is not lost, for with our tears we can water roses. Upon your return, please use this mirror to contact us.

Zel"

"What in the blazes is a Zel?" Sigmund grumbled, snatching the paper from Grim's hands.

But Dagobert, Sigurd, and Grim were already racing out the door, followed closely by the others, around the corner of the house to the garden. Something shone in the cold moonlight from above as they tramped through the snow.

It was a coffin, the bottom made of carved, gleaming gold, the top a rounded dome of pure glass so it could be viewed from all sides. And there, inside of it on a bed of white satin, lay Makellos, dressed in his fine princely garb, hands folded atop his chest, head of dark hair resting on a plump pillow, looking for all the world like he had fallen asleep under the stars in the garden he loved so much and would wake any moment. A sleeping beauty, the fairest of them all. They all stared at the elaborate entombment for a very long time, nothing moving but the puffs of breath coming from their lips.

"What does this mean?" Bernhardt finally asked. "Who could have done this?"

"Perhaps the mirror mentioned in the note shall give us the answer," said Hardwic. They all glanced between one another, for no one had thought to grab the mirror or even look for it. They all trooped back inside to the warmth once more, finding a small handheld looking glass atop the pile of blankets.

Grim snatched it up, holding it up in front of his face. "Hullo? Who's there?" he growled. For a moment, its silver surface only reflected his own face and sharply pointed beard, and a few of the other faces trying to crowd around him to see. After a moment, it began to swirl, as if with dark, black smoke, and two faces appeared.

One was pale and fair-haired, with a face nearly as lovely as their own lost prince, eyes shimmering a brilliant green. The other was a taller, darker figure with pointed elven ears, with hair as black as Makellos', but it seemed to be infused with stars that twinkled and glittered like the tiniest diamonds in the mine's walls.

"Ulrich," breathed Der, peering over Grim's shoulder. He had heard the name many times before, long ago when he as an apothecary had created elixirs and remedies, though his own were not at all magical. The legendary sorcerer had hoarded many books on forbidden magic that were thought lost, including those with knowledge on plants and herbal concoctions not seen elsewhere in centuries. There was no one else that the dark-haired figure could be.

"What is an Ulrich?" asked Bernhardt, who was stuck behind the others trying to see.

Grim glared into the mirror. "I assume we have you to thank for breaking into our house?"

"And the coffin," Ulrich agreed, not seeming at all perturbed by Grim's accusation. "Though that should only be a temporary measure."

"What are you talking about?" Grim snarled. "You have some nerve coming into our home and touching the prin-" Hardwic gave him a sharp elbow to the ribs.

"Thank you for your kindness, sir," he said politely to the mirror. "And I assume yours as well," he said with a nod to the fair creature with the brilliant eyes and hair.

The youth's lips curved into a warm smile. "I am glad to help. My name is Zel."

Grim let out a snort. "I don't care who you are. What is it you want from us?"

"Don't mind him," Der said with a glower at Grim. "We are all on edge after what happened to the prince."

"Yes, I assumed that," said Ulrich, still in his calm way. "What do *you* believe happened?"

"We think he was killed by the Queen," said Der.

"Of course he was," Grim snarled.

"You would be correct," Ulrich replied, and next to him, Zel looked a little sad. "But every magic spell can be broken in some way."

"Even in death?" piped up old Bernhardt.

"Even in death," Ulrich repeated. "We shall find a way to break this spell over the prince, if that is what you wish."

"Yes!" said Hardwic, followed by a rousing agreement from everyone, even Grim.

"But what will you do once the prince is restored?" asked Zel. "The Queen has killed him once. She would not hesitate to do it again."

There was a rustle of movement and mutters amongst the seven. Zel was right; if they brought Makellos back, they would constantly have to be on their guard for the Queen's return. Even if they sent him south, over the mountains, he might not be safe, and they could not bear to never see him again anyway.

"That witch has destroyed so much in this kingdom," Grim growled. "I would see her dead before I let her harm a hair on Snow's head again."

"As would I," said Sigurd.

"And I," added Sigmund.

"Dead," agreed Dagobert, surprising everyone with how strong his soft voice was.

"Then heed my words," Ulrich said, his voice dropping even lower. "I will find the antidote to the spell that has taken the prince's life, but you must be steadfast in your resolve to kill the Queen. For once he is revived, her rage will be swift and terrible, and she will know that it is I who helped you. I hold no love in my heart for Schön; I would see her end, but I am not as powerful as I once was and unable to do it myself."

Der looked between the other six miners, each one's face set in dark determination. They had lost so much at the hands of Queen Schön; the glimmer of hope that their dear prince could be restored to them and that the kingdom might be freed once and for all from her tyranny was all they needed. "We'll be ready," he said, turning back to the mirror.

Ulrich nodded. "Very well. We shall arrive in a few days, once we have determined the limits of the magic and have reached out to the Thieves Guild. They will be more than willing to help you in this quest."

And then, the mirror went dark again. For a moment, no one spoke. Then Grim said, "So, I guess we're fucking killing the Queen."

Nineteen

It was indeed several long, excruciating days before they heard from the old sorcerer again. At least having to carry on with work as though nothing had happened was not an unfamiliar task. Each morning, they all came to the coffin to tell Makellos good morning, and at the end of the day, they bid him good night. Whomever stayed home to take care of things would check on him and very often find the tracks of animals in the snow around the coffin. Squirrels, rabbits, birds, deer, all manner of forest-dwelling creatures had come to pay their respects to the fallen prince, it seemed. And through it all, Makellos remained asleep, as still as stone, though his body did not waste away. He seemed but to slumber peacefully under the cold winter sun.

Hardwic was the one tending the home late in the afternoon when Zel and Ulrich arrived, bundled in furs against the cold, though he had not heard them approach through the trees. He invited them in and offered them tea and ginger cookies from the market until such time as his companions made their way home from work. They all gathered around the table expectantly, Zel and Ulrich at the head.

Ulrich reached into his pocket and withdrew something small that he set before them. It was the apple that had been on the floor where Makellos had fallen, ignored and forgotten in their grief, with the single bite out of it. "The Sleeping Death," he announced without preamble. "No doubt the Queen assumed he would be buried, or burnt upon a pyre, never having awoken again."

"Well, dead is still dead, so what's the antidote?" Grim asked with a pointed glare. The others seemed aghast that he was so rude to the mighty sorcerer and his companion in their midst.

But Zel merely laughed and pulled out a rolled-up piece of parchment from a pocket, spreading it out next to the apple. "The victim of the Sleeping Death spell may be revived by True Love's Kiss."

The seven little men looked amongst themselves in confusion. "Must it be upon the lips?" asked Der.

Zel raised a perfectly sculpted brow. "There is no stipulation as such."

"Then why hasn't he revived?" Sigurd demanded. "We have all kissed him goodbye."

"And we love him," Sigmund added. "Surely there is not one of us who loves him more than the others."

"Did we not love him enough?" lamented Hardwic, his usually cheery countenance falling into a dissolution of tears.

"Of course we did," Grimwald snapped. "We loved him, and he loved us. There has to be something we're missing."

"Did he perhaps have a first love?" Bernhardt asked helplessly. "An unrequited love or lover scorned?"

That sent grumbles and mutters through the group, each voice growing louder and more intense, as such that when Dagobert raised his hand, none of them noticed for several seconds. When they finally did, and silence fell once more, Dagobert said softly, "I didn't."

"Didn't what?" Der asked gently. The others all leaned in with wide eyes, as though disbelieving that the young man could not have loved the sweet prince.

"Kiss him." Dagobert's voice had dropped to a whisper. "The guards came."

Each of them thought back to that horrible day when the guards had broken down their door and they had hidden Makellos beneath their blankets on the very table they currently sat at. Each remembered pressing a kiss to the prince's hands, lips, forehead, cheek, as they shared in their collective grief. But no one could recall Dagobert, the weepy last of them to come forward, completing the same embrace.

"Well, what are we waiting for?" Grimwald said, leaping to his feet. And he ran out the front door into the icy winter without cloak or covering. There was a scramble as the six others followed after him, tailed by Ulrich and Zel. They all hurried out to the garden, the glass of the coffin shining under the starlight, the only real source of light.

Sigurd and Grim lifted the glass lid from the coffin and set it aside, and then all gathered round to gaze at the sleeping prince, still so peaceful in his bed of satin.

Dagobert swallowed and stepped forward, but Hardwic held up a hand. "Wait."

"We've waited long enough," Grimwald snapped.

"I know. But should we perhaps... all kiss him again? If Dagobert alone kisses and awakens him, might that present a question as to whether he is the most beloved amongst the lot of us?"

There was an uncomfortable silence as the seven little men exchanged looks. Each was suddenly realizing the truth in Hardwic's words. Makellos had never shown favor to any one of them over another; that did not mean that there might not be one particular favorite in his heart. But that was his own secret to keep, not theirs to be inferred from a single moment. At least if they all kissed the prince, there was equality between them.

"I think that is fair," Bernhardt said with a nod.

So, they all lined up, one by one, from eldest to youngest, Dagobert at the end of the line. Bernhardt pressed a kiss to Makellos' lips, then stepped aside for Der, Hardwic, Grimwald, Sigurd, and Sigmund. Last came Dagobert, kneeling by the coffin's base. He stroked a hand over Makellos' cheek, still so soft even in death. His tears fell upon the prince's enchanted clothes and immediately dried. He leaned down and pressed a soft kiss to the sinful, pink lips that he had kissed so many times before.

The silence of the night felt like a living thing as all nine of those gathered stared down at the prince in the coffin. And then, the softest rustle of clothing, the smallest intake of breath. Makellos' blue eyes, the one as clear and shining as a cloudless summer sky, slowly opened, staring up at nothing at first, as if unsure what he was seeing. He blinked a few times, and then his whole body slowly stirred to life, hands unfolding from one another on his torso, limbs stretching as if awakening from a long slumber.

He turned his head to the side and found Dagobert staring at him in wide-eyed shock. He blinked, taking a deep breath of crisp, sweet forest air. "What's wrong?" he asked gently, pushing himself up from where he had been lying down. It was cold, he realized, very cold, and the ground was covered in a layer of fluffy snow. They were in the garden, he realized. Had he been asleep? But why was he sleeping in the garden, of all places?

Dagobert's eyes were as round and wide as saucers. His hand with its stubby fingers reached out and touched Makellos' cheek, then patted over it, as if the man were a specter who was not completely solid. But yet he was. The warmth had returned to his skin, the blush of the rose upon his cheek and lips once more. "You... were dead," he said in his soft, sweet way, still staring at Makellos in disbelief.

The words took him by surprise, and he cast his mind back to his last memory. Sitting in the cottage, a bright red apple in his hand. An old crone in black talking with him as he bit into the luscious scarlet fruit. And then, nothing. Had death really come for him?

He realized then that he was surrounded, the other six miners and two strangers standing nearby, all staring at him. And then one of the miners let out a joyous whoop that echoed off of the surrounding trees and sent night birds scattering into the sky, and suddenly they were all shouting and cheering and crying. He found his arms full of Dagobert and Bernhardt, the others pressing in around him, peppering his face and hair with kisses and tears.

"Let him breathe, let him breathe," Der said after a long moment, and most of the men loosened their grips on Makellos.

"Get him inside, it's freezing out here," Hardwic chided. For the first time, everyone seemed to realize the cold, and they ushered Makellos quickly back into the cottage, placing him by the fire wrapped in a blanket and pouring him a mug of tea.

Once he was settled in place, Makellos found himself facing the two strangers who were standing off to the side, the dark-haired man's arms wrapped protectively around the blond as they watched.

He stared at the glittering universe in the taller man's hair. "You must be Ulrich."

The man smiled and gave him a small bow. "Indeed I am, your highness. And my beloved, Zel."

"A pleasure to meet you, Prince Makellos," said Zel with a nod that made the fair youth's golden braid swish into clearer view, proving nearly long enough to brush the floor.

"Prince Makellos is dead," the young man said with a small smile. "Until such time as he is able to return to seize the throne from the evil Queen, he is still cold and lifeless. I am Snow White."

Twenty

"We haven't much time," Ulrich said a little later as they all sat on the benches near the fire, nursing more tea and cookies. "Schön will rise at dawn, and soon thereafter will learn that her son lives."

"We are prepared to fight," Sigurd said firmly.

"Yes. If you can get us inside the castle, we're ready to kill the Queen," Sigmund added.

Snow glanced around. He had only just come back to them. Slipping into the palace was dangerous, even for the most cunning and brave of men. He did not want to risk losing any of them, not when he had been granted such an extraordinary second chance at life. "I do not wish you to risk your lives for mine," he said softly. "Please."

"As long as the Queen lives, you are in danger," Grim said, his voice full of dark promise. "We will protect you in any way."

"But you are not killers," Snow said softly. "I do not wish to put that burden upon any of you. Not for my sake."

"Not just for you," said Bernhardt, his wise eyes on the mug of tea in his tiny hands. "For everything we have had taken from us. Our homes, our families, our lives."

"We have never had the chance or the will to strike back," Hardwic said, taking one of Snow's hands and giving it a squeeze. "If we are ever to do it, it must be now. While we have friends and allies." He turned his cheery smile toward Ulrich and Zel.

Snow glanced around the room as the other miners murmured their agreement, trying to think of what they could do. An uprising would involve planning, and they had limited time to do so. And open rebellion could result in innocent people being hurt.

Something caught his eye. Something red and shiny. He rose to his feet, slipping through the assemblage and over to the table. Upon it still sat the apple with the singular bite out of it, and, next to it, the page Zel had laid down that described the effects and the antidote. He read it over, aware that all eyes were on his back, watching his every move. There was a collective inhale from the little men as his fingers closed around the apple, still as red and perfect as it had been when his mother, in her peddler disguise, had first handed it to him. He lifted it up to study it. It looked to be such a simple, innocent thing. Small, but deadly, the way his coterie of lovers was. If there was a way to make it even smaller...

He turned to the group, his eyes landing on Der. "Would you be able to turn this into a powder?"

Der blinked at the question, glancing from side to side at the others, as if unsure whether Snow was addressing him, before he cleared his throat. "I should think so. It would have to be dried first."

"Easily magically accomplished," said Zel with a sly smile. "What did you have in mind, Snow?"

Snow's lips formed a devious little smirk that he turned on Zel and Ulrich. "If you can get me safely into the castle, I know a way to kill my mother, and none of us will have to lift a single finger."

Ulrich's own smile mirrored Zel's crafty one. "The Thieves Guild is at your service. Just tell us what you need."

Dawn was just breaking over the horizon when Ulrich transported Zel, Snow, and the seven miners to just outside of the Thieves Guild in the town. One moment they were standing in the miners' cottage; the next, the sounds and scents of the streets of Falchovari greeted them. Grimwald crossed his arms. "Huh. It ain't natural," he said with a small glower at Ulrich.

The sorcerer only smiled one of his mysterious smiles. "Neither am I."

Dagobert turned in a wide circle. He had been so young when he was taken from his family, he had hardly any memory outside of the mines. The houses and shops were so tall and close together, almost like trees in a forest, and there were shops with beautiful glass windows displaying everything from baked goods to fabric to tools. He pressed his face up against a window to stare at a pair of finely crafted ruby red leather shoes on display there. He had never seen anything so elegant or bright.

Snow smiled and leaned down next to him. "If all goes well, we'll be able to get you as many fancy shoes as you want." Dagobert giggled and nodded, touching Snow's blue waistcoat, then grabbing at his own tunic with a haughty air and a look down his nose in his imitation of the Queen. Snow laughed, and it was the most beautiful sound Dagobert had ever heard.

They all met with Zel's parents, Gregor and Sophie, the newest heads of the Thieves Guild since the recent unseating of the previous leader, Lothar. There was a crew of Thieves Guild members ready to help them, especially after Snow shared his plan to kill the Queen. One of the members, introduced as a whisperer, was rather scarily familiar with the interior of the palace, including its hidden entrances and weak points. Snow made it a point in his mind to never find himself on the wrong side of the Thieves Guild if this plan worked.

As the populace began to rise and come to life, the group dispersed. Snow, Grim, Der, and their whisperer guide headed one way, toward the palace. The other little men, along with members of the Guild, circulated into the streets. They knocked on doors and stepped into shops. "The Queen wishes to make a royal announcement at noon. It is requested that all who are willing and able please assemble outside of the streets in front of the palace." The word spread quickly through the town, which buzzed like bees in a hive. The Queen so rarely made an appearance to her subjects; she had always acted as though they were beneath her. An announcement in person could either be very good or very, very bad. Most of the townsfolk suspected the latter.

S now, Der, Grim, and their whisperer guide slipped silently into a drain and followed it from its exit into a river, back along its path. The tunnel was not tall enough for Snow or the whisperer to stand fully upright, though Der and Grim had no trouble. It stank of sewage, and Snow had a dark feeling in his heart as they followed it, for he thought he knew where its egress was.

"This is as far as I go," said the whisperer when they reached a locked gate that the whisperer was easily able to open for them.

Der, Grim, and Snow stepped out of the gate and into the dimness of the dungeon below the castle. There were only a few windows, scattered high along the walls, so high that they were not easily accessible from inside, and they were relatively small as well. Individual cells were made from stone, with heavy, wooden doors closing them in, making it impossible to tell how many of them were actually occupied. Snow could smell must and mildew and unwashed bodies, and it nearly made him retch. He had only been to the dungeons a few times in his life; they had scared him so terribly as a child that he avoided them and often pretended that they did not actually exist. He realized now how foolish that was of him; people were down here in these cells, suffering, many for 'crimes' that were nothing more than an inability to provide tax to the Queen, or stealing food and clothing for their children. His tender heart ached. No one deserved to be sent to the dungeons for lack of necessities. He could no longer turn a blind eye to the suffering of those around him.

The Thieves Guild had provided him with information about the castle, and deep within the shadows of the dungeon, they found a back stairwell that spiraled upwards into darkness. Der lit a torch to help them navigate the steep, stone stairs, keeping its flame low, though Snow suspected that no one more living than a few rats had used these stairs in many years, for they were covered with cobwebs and a layer of dust that almost could have passed for fallen snow.

As they climbed up the steep stairs, Snow wondered if they might fall down them to their deaths. He wouldn't be surprised if this was the most treacherous part of the entire quest and also explained why these stairs were not more commonly used. Up they climbed, each step feeling like they were ascending into the lair of a giant, until they reached what seemed to be a door at the top of the staircase. There was a latch on the inside that Grim unlocked by the light of Der's torch. Der then smothered the flames, and they pushed the little door open to peek out.

It was the guest wing of the palace, rarely used nowadays, and not far from the wing that housed his own chambers and those of the Queen. There were no servants or guards about, so Snow gestured for Der and Grim to follow him out of the hidden doorway, closing it behind them so it blended into the wall once more.

Down the hallway they crept on cautious feet, passing no one but a few silent portraits of nobles on the walls, who had nothing to say in the matter of their invasion. They reached the end of the wing. Snow peeked out, then ducked back in, holding his finger to his lips in silence as several guards came hurrying down the hall, stopping in front of the closed door of the Queen's chambers. One of them lifted his hand to knock, but before he could, the door was yanked open, and Queen Schön came flying out into the hallway in a flurry of purple and black fabric, her blond hair bouncing on her shoulders. She nearly ran into the guards, who took a hasty step backwards. "What is going on?" she demanded.

"We're not sure, your majesty," said one of the guards nervously, glancing sideways at the other guards to see if they had a better answer. "The people seem to be gathering in the town square."

"Is the prince with them?" she demanded, her voice unnaturally shrill.

"Prince Makellos?" the guard asked in surprise. "I... don't know, your majesty. But we've been assigned to protect you."

Queen Schön rolled her eyes. "Well, come on then." She huffed and stormed down the hall, the guards hurrying after her. As soon as they rounded the corner, Snow gestured to Der and Grim. "Come on." They hurried into the Queen's private chambers, where an elegant four-poster bed sat, perfectly fixed by the servants. Her vanity with her makeup and a large mirror was across the room by an ornately-styled window. Everywhere there glinted gemstones of every size, shape, and color, from the eyes of animals carved on furniture, to jewelry on her vanity and dressing table, to even imbedded within the walls. It was almost like being within an oversized treasure box. Der found himself momentarily distracted, staring around open-mouthed at the finery laid out before them, turning in a slow circle to take it all in.

"Shut yer mouth, you look like a landed fish," Grim whisper-snapped, grabbing Der by the collar and yanking him forward. "Where is this secret workshop?"

Against one wall was the elegantly crafted armoire, with its beautifully inlaid mosaic of gemstones in the pattern of a great peacock, plumage extended, glittering with sapphires and emeralds. Snow gave the doors a pull but found them locked, as he suspected. His heart picked up. They had to get inside, or this would all be for naught. "I know it's behind these doors."

"Shall I break them down?" Grim said, hefting his ax over his shoulder.

Snow cringed. Chopping through wardrobe doors would be extremely loud and might bring the guards running. He ran his fingers over the gemstones, trying to press each one. "One of these has to unlock the doors, I'm sure of it. I just don't know which one."

Grim began to press at the gemstones with his thumb as well. "There has to be a thousand of them. We'll be at this for an hour."

"Oh no, we won't," said Der thoughtfully. He reached into a little bag at his hip, pulling out a thin, pointy piece of metal no thicker than a quill. He knelt down by the floor and slid the pointed tip of it into the hinge of the door. He gave it a hard push with his knee, and the lynchpin popped up. He stood and wiggled it out of the hinge, setting it aside, then held up the pointed tool to Snow. "And the top one?"

Snow grinned, leaning down to give him a sweet kiss on the lips. "You're a genius, Der!"

Der flushed as Snow took the metal tool and poked it up into the upper hinge. Grim let out a huff. "Well, nobody likes a showoff."

The second lynchpin popped up, and Snow pulled it free. The heavy door began to sag, now only supported by the hinge plates balancing precariously on top of one another, and the lock still in place holding the two doors. He dug his fingers into the wood and pulled the door so the hinge pieces slid free of one another, and the door swung to the side. But it didn't open very far, as the lock still held the two heavy doors bolted together.

"Allow me," said Grim, eyeing the tiny gap formed by the sagging door. Snow and Der stepped aside as Grim raised his ax, adjusted his stance, and brought the ax blade down between the doors, cutting through the peg that held them fast. The heavy, decorated door separated from its mate with a loud crack and then hit the floor with a resounding thunk. Snow and Der shoved it aside, not caring where it ended up.

"Thank you, Grim," Snow said, dropping another kiss onto the grumpy man's lips. Grim smirked back, and the three of them slipped inside the armoire.

Torches on the walls burst into flame to light the room they entered. It was circular, and quite large, with ancient parchments and texts on the walls. Dusty books were scattered on shelves crudely cut into the stone walls. The floor was also stone. Against one wall was a large, gilded mirror that stood as tall as Snow himself. What looked to be a human skull sat on the worktable, staring vacantly at them from its empty eye sockets, teeth grinning a hideous smile. There were all manner of devices and objects that he had no idea what they were for, presumably magical uses. He was sure Ulrich would know.

All around them, stones glittered. In boxes, on tabletops, in precarious piles. Some Snow could identify, but many others he could not. There were gemstone rocks in every color of the rainbow, some still in a crude state directly from the mines, others carved and polished into beautifully cut stones or carved figurines. But there were no precious stones to be seen. Ulrich had informed him that the purest diamonds, rubies, emeralds, and sapphires, the ones that came from the southern foothill mountain mines, were what gave the Queen her powers, and those were the ones she crushed to create her magical potion. The one she had developed while still under Ulrich's tutelage, that prolonged her life and her beauty. She drank it every morning, so he was sure it would be easy to spot. And, indeed, it was.

The glass bottle of shimmering, silver powder sat proudly on the wooden worktable. A mortar and pestle lay next to it where the Queen ground the gemstones from the mine where the little men were forced to dig each day. Every drop of blood that had been spilled in that horrific place was because of his mother's vanity. The bottle was nearly empty; she would be brewing a new batch soon.

He had no idea how much powder was needed for her daily elixir, so he just scooped some into a small cut glass vial nearby, adding some water from a bowl to liquefy it.He turned to Der, giving him a small smile. "Ready."

Into his hand, Der placed a small packet of powder. It looked like nothing at all, but it held the weight of the kingdom inside. Snow undid the twine binding it closed and opened it. Careful to keep the powder off of his hands, he tipped the packet into the vial. The slightly pinkish powder slid into the silver mixture. He put the cork back in place and gave it a shake to mix it. When he looked in it again, the powder had blended into the mirror-like silver depths that gleamed like shimmering stars. It was beautiful and deadly. Like his mother. Like him. He picked up the larger bottle with the remaining silver powder in it, holding it out to Grimwald. "Smash this?"

"Gladly," Grim said, setting down his ax and taking the bottle in both hands. He raised it above his head, looking up at Snow with a small, dark smile. "For all of the lives that bitch destroyed." Then he brought his arms downward with all of his might, casting the bottle as if swinging an ax into a chunk of wood. The bottle hit the stone floor and exploded, glass tinkling like the ringing of tiny bells. The silver powder inside spread across the floor and into the cracks between the stones like grains of sand. Despite there being no windows in this room, a cold draft seemed to catch the powdered gemstones and scatter them until they were no more than a glittery layer of fine dust.

And now, they just needed the Queen to return.

"That felt good. Mind if I smash a few more things?" Grim asked, glancing around the room at all of the many vials and pottery.

"Have at it," Snow said. "I've got what we need." And the noise would probably get his mother's attention.

Grim grinned and picked up another glass bottle, throwing it against the far wall where it shattered into pieces with another sharp crash.

Snow stepped up to the gilded mirror on the wall, gazing into its silver depths that reflected him and Der and Grim. He reached up to brush his fingers over its polished surface, wondering if that was how his mother had been able to find him.

"What wouldst thou know, my prince?" intoned a voice that made all three of them jump. Snow looked around before realizing the voice seemed to have come from the mirror itself.

"Jiminy crickets, a talking mirror!" Der gasped, adjusting his spectacles as if he were not actually seeing it.

"What can you tell me?" Snow asked the mirror, suddenly curious. "Can you tell me the future?"

"I can only speak the truth," the mirror replied solemnly. "The future is not yet determined, so there is no truth in it."

Snow did not allow himself to become disappointed. Even if the mirror had been able to tell him what the future held, he wasn't entirely sure he wanted to know. If their plan succeeded, the weight of the kingdom would fall upon his shoulders, and there would be many decisions to be made, not the least of which was whether he remained in power. He couldn't even be sure that the townspeople would not string him up or exile him from the land, as the son of the evil Queen who had tormented them for so long.

"There is one thing I wish to know," he said softly, and he was aware that Der was silently watching him and Grim had paused in his smashing of the bottles.

"Then ask," the mirror replied.

"Am I worthy of being king?"

"You have doubt in your heart," the mirror said. "But the fact that you question your worthiness shows that you have a fair heart, the fairest in the land. Worth is not measured by beauty or gold, but by being fearless, fair, brave, and true. You are all of these things, and you are worthy of being king."

Snow felt warm all over, aware that Der had slipped his hand into his and squeezed it tightly, and that Grim was still watching them from the nearby table. He had a good heart; the fairest, the mirror had said. Even should he not be king, he was still a good person, which was enough for him. "Thank you," he said to the mirror.

There was a sudden sharp creak and snap from the area of the door they had entered. Snow looked up to see Queen Schön in the doorway, resplendent in a gown of deep purple, her gold, bejeweled crown atop her perfectly coiffed hair. The perfection of it was countered by the look of absolute rage marring her beautiful face as her blue eyes surveyed the wreckage of her magic.

"What have you done?" The sound was unlike any he had ever heard from his mother, her melodious tone now a feral-sounding growl through clenched teeth. He thought that, in that moment, if his mother had been able to transform into a creature with massive claws and fangs, she would have and would then have ripped him into tiny pieces. For just a moment, he was afraid. This was a woman who had killed him once before. Who had destroyed the lives of his lovers and their families. Had laughed while children cried and died of hunger in the streets. She was not to be underestimated, for her cruelty knew no bounds.

But then he felt Der and Grimwald straighten up on either side of him, strong as massive oak trees. They were ready to fight for him. For this kingdom. For everything they had lost. For everything they might lose again. He would not let them down, and he would not allow this awful, heartless woman to bring further harm to them.

"Hello, Mother," he said, giving her an impish little smile, though his voice trembled just the tiniest bit. "You are looking beautiful as always."

"Makellos," the Queen growled, the sound low in her chest like that of bear or tiger.

Snow held up the shimmering glass vial in his hand so the Queen could see it. "Is this what you drink every day?" His voice was a bit steadier now. He could hear her inhale, see the flicker of recognition in her blue eyes. She swept her cold gaze over the shambles of her potions, the broken glass upon the floor and the shimmering layer of her ground gemstones that coated it. "I seem to have broken the large bottle. I always was so clumsy, wasn't I?"

"You impudent little fool," Schön said, narrowing her eyes at him. "What game are you playing at?"

"No game," Snow said. "But this does appear to be the last of it."

"And the miners have gone on strike," said Der suddenly.

Grim took a step forward on his other side, his dark eyes full of murderous rage. "You ain't gettin' another swing of a pickaxe from any of us, unless it's through your skull."

The Queen's countenance suddenly morphed. She straightened up, lifted her chin, and gave Snow a familiar cold look down her regal nose, a bemused chuckle escaping her lips. "Oh, my. Look at your gallant defenders, *Snow White*. Together, they very nearly make a whole man. How simply adorable." Her voice had returned to its usual musical coo, dripping with venom. She stepped fully inside the chamber, between them and the door. "Well now. Here we are. No guards, no games, no disguises. Just mother and son, and a few… minor problems to be eliminated."

Snow took a deep breath, his heart hammering in his chest. "I'll smash it," he threatened, giving the vial a shake so the silver liquid sloshed and gleamed. "And you will not be able to make more without your precious jewels."

Schön laughed. "Oh, my dear, do you think I will not find others to work the mines? I can be quite persuasive."

"I have an idea," said Grim with a sly little smirk up at Snow. "*You* should drink the potion, your highness. You are already fairer than your withered old hag of a mother. You have even defeated death. And every day you will become more beautiful, while the ugly old Queen fades away and is forgotten."

"What a lovely idea!" Der said. "I like it."

"I like it as well," Snow said, turning his sunny smile upon them both. He held up the bottle even as his heart beat a tattoo in his ears.

"You shall never be fairer than I!" the Queen screeched, flinging herself across the space at Snow. Her fingers, nails sharp as claws, extended in a grasp. For his face or for the bottle, he did not know. He only knew when the Queen's nails raked across his cheek in a path of fire. His head snapped to the side, taking his body with it, and he went sprawling on the stone floor. The impact caused the vial to fly from his hand and hit the floor with a ring like a funeral bell, and his heart nearly stopped. If the cork had come loose or the vial had shattered, they would be done for.

"Snow, are you all right?" Grim asked as the Queen stumbled past them and dropped to hands and knees to scoop up the gleaming container from the floor.

"Yes," Snow said, pulling his hand away from his cheek to see several droplets of bright red blood on his fingers. His head pounded, and his cheek stung, but he didn't care right now. All that mattered was the vial.

Queen Schön laughed, the sound low and menacing as she rose to her feet, brushing off her majestic purple dress with one hand. She held up the vial in the other, and Snow was relieved to see the stopper still in place. He pushed himself up to his knees, reaching up a hand desperately, though she was far beyond his grasp. The Queen flicked off the cork top with a long, elegant finger, and it went rolling across the floor. She raised the vial to her blood-red lips, giving Snow a self-satisfied smirk as she opened her mouth and swallowed the shimmering contents in one gulp. Snow could see the mouthful flow down her throat like a snake swallowing a mouse. Then the Queen dropped the vial to the ground. It shattered into a thousand little glass particles, and the Queen ground her foot on top of it until it was nothing but dust. "Poor little prince," she cooed, her ruby lips curving into a smile as sweet as lemons. "You tried so hard to escape me, but it's too late now. You and your deplorable little beasts will never live to see another sunrise. You could never become fairer than I. You are just a shadow, a reflection in the mirror, a-"

Queen Schön suddenly froze, one hand flying to her stomach, the other pressing to her breast above her heart. Her icy features went slack, her already pale face seeming to drain of all color entirely. "What... what is happening?"

Makellos smiled as he pushed himself up to his feet with assistance from Der and Grim. "Where do you imagine the rest of the poisoned apple you used on me went, Mother?"

Schön looked at him with wide eyes, her inky pupils nearly blotting out the blue. "What did you do?" she hissed.

Makellos straightened his back, as he had always been told to do when addressing anyone. A bead of crimson blood from his cheek landed on his white collar and immediately faded away. "I should be surprised that you did not notice the smell of apple in your potion, but I suppose that speaks to the talent of those who formulated it, as well as the greed with which you consumed it." Der straightened his back proudly at that.

The Queen snarled, anger replacing fear on her sculpted face. "You ungrateful, disgusting whelp! How dare you!" She snatched up the potion book from the tabletop, fumbling its heavy cover with shaking hands. She frantically turned the mouldering pages, ripping many of them in her haste and incoordination.

"There is an antidote, Mother. You know that," Makellos said, watching her with a devious smile. "The poison may be reversed by True Love's Kiss. But there is no one who truly loves you. Even I, your own flesh and blood, do not have enough love in my heart to reverse the magic you have inflicted upon yourself."

The Queen dropped the book with a heavy thunk, stumbling against the table, sending bottles and bowls sloshing and spilling. Der and Grim still held their positions firmly in front of Makellos, sturdy as stone statues, as Schön turned to him again, her face gone a ghastly shade of gray.

"And so," Makellos continued, "you shall sleep. You shall sleep in your grave amongst the rot and worms, as the kingdom recovers from your spite and cruelty. You shall sleep until the world forgets that you ever existed and the walls you built have crumbled into dust."

The Queen stepped forward, opening her mouth in a shriek full of all of her malice and hatred. Makellos recoiled before he saw that under her fine dress, her feet had suddenly turned into a fine powder. She let out another scream, this one an other-worldly sound, toppling forward as her legs became no more solid than gritty sand. The glittering powder moved rapidly up her torso, over her chest and into her arms. Her hand with its perfectly manicured nails and bejeweled rings reached out toward his face again, but the diamond dust slid down her hand, into each finger. The last bit of it turned to dust just as her longest fingernail brushed his cheek. For a moment, she stood, suspended in time, a glittering edifice in a royal gown and golden crown, her beautiful face twisted into a scream of rage, before her body suddenly began to crumble and melt as a sandcastle before a tide. Rivulets of gleaming dust streamed off of her, her fingers breaking off and hitting the floor with a soft thump. The next moment, Queen Schön's body had fallen, and then there lay on the floor only her fine clothes and jewelry alongside her bejeweled crown, draped over a heap of dark, shimmering diamond dust. The evil Queen Schön was no more.

Grim coughed and waved his hand in front of him to clear the powder that had wafted from the pile of what amounted to not more than ashes on the floor. "Well, that was unexpected."

Makellos turned to Der with a confused stare. The poisoned apple in her potion was meant to put her to sleep, not dissolve her, though he supposed the outcome was essentially the same. "What happened?"

Der took off his glasses, wiping them on the hem of his tunic as he squinted at the pile of diamond dust in front of him. "I don't know. Fascinating. Perhaps there was just so much evil in her, the poison reacted to it. Magic kept her alive for so long, it may have created a backlash."

"Well, good riddance, says I," said Grim with a snort. He stepped over to the pile, kicking aside the dress and surrounding fine grains of diamond powder so he could pick up the golden crown. He blew on it a few times to clear the dust off of it before he turned around and held it out to Makellos. "Your majesty."

Makellos stared at it in mute surprise, as if he had never seen it before. The silence lasted for so long that Grim let out an uneasy cough. "I ain't gettin' down on one knee. I'm short enough as it is."

That broke whatever had transfixed Makellos, and he took the crown in his hands with a bark of laughter. "Thank you, Grim. I… will find out from my people if that is what they want."

They made their way out of the Queen's chambers and through the castle. Many of the guards were occupied with standing toward the front of the castle as the townspeople gathered for what they thought would be an announcement from the Queen. Makellos received many surprised looks from the few guards and servants they passed, as well as many grateful and pleased smiles, especially when they saw the Queen's crown in his hand. He suspected many of them had thought him dead and seemed relieved that he was not. He gave them all smiles back, bidding the servants to follow him to the main gates.

When he arrived at the palace doors, they were opened, and he stepped out into the courtyard to find a large gathering of the town waiting expectantly in the street as the guards all stood at the gates. They parted as he drew near to them, bowing. A few steps behind him, Grim smirked at the guards.

At the castle gates, Makellos lifted the crown high above his head so everyone could see it. "Citizens of Falchovari," he said, his sweet voice carrying across the open air. "My mother, Queen Schön, is dead."

There was a stunned silence as people stared at him, then blankly at one another. The cold, cruel Queen had ruled Falchovari for two hundred years; it was all they had known. Then, in the silence, Dagobert gave a delighted whoop. And then there were cheers and applause and laughter and crying all bubbling up at once. People tossed their hats into the air. Husbands embraced their wives and children. One elderly man toward the front of the crowd began to dance a jig. The streets echoed with the sounds of newfound freedom.

This went on for some minutes before it started to die down, and Makellos lifted his voice once more. "Many of you may not know me. I am Prince Makellos. Queen Schön was my mother, but not my family. Her reign of treachery and cruelty ends with her. She poisoned everyone into believing that it's everyone for themselves. But I intend to spend every day of my life from here on out earning your trust and bettering our fair kingdom, restoring it, caring for those who are most in need, and creating a better future for our descendants. But whether that is as your king or something else, I leave that up to you, the good people of Falchovari, to decide."

A rustle went through the crowd again. Makellos felt his heart pick up in his chest. He knew he was asking a lot. Many of them had never seen him before, and knowing who his mother was, he would understand if the people decided they did not wish to have the son of the evil Queen as their ruler. He just had to hope that if they did not want him to rule, they would not choose violence.

Someone stepped to the front of the crowd, face hidden by a thick, brown cloak. But when he stepped up next to Hardwic and Bernhardt and pulled his hood back, Makellos nearly wept for joy to see Hans, the kindly huntsman who had spared his life. Hans gazed back at him with his dark eyes before he pressed his hand to his chest and lowered himself to one knee. "I pledge my loyalty to King Makellos," he said, his voice thick with emotion.

"As do I," said Sigurd a few steps away, bowing at the waist.

"And I," added Sigmund, mirroring the bow.

"And I," said Dagobert in the strongest voice Makellos had ever heard from him.

There was a wave of movement through the crowd as most of them bowed at least their heads to him. Makellos felt his heart warm, his cheeks rosy. The kingdom seemed to be overwhelmingly supporting him.

One of the guards looked uncertainly at Hans, then at Makellos. "Your Hi- Your Majesty, we are under orders to arrest Hans upon sight."

Hans looked up from his bow, his face pinched in a worried frown. Makellos smiled calmly. "Then, as my first official act, I pardon Hans for whatever crimes he might have committed that were determined by my mother. He is a free man."

A cheer went up from the crowd. Makellos swept his eyes over seven little men standing at the front of the group, the men who had come to mean so much to him, who had protected him at the risk of their own lives, whom he loved with all of his heart. "And my second official act, all enforced exiles and servitudes will be revoked, and every prison sentence commanded by the former Queen shall be re-evaluated in a timely manner."

Hardwic, Sigurd, Sigmund, Grimwald, and Dagobert let out a cheer of delight that the crowd echoed, while Bernhardt wiped tears from his eyes, and Der smiled proudly at Makellos.

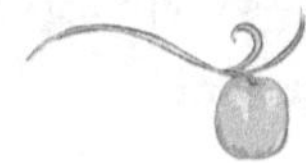

"Well, now, it seems that you've come a long way from our little shack in the woods, your majesty," Bernhardt said with a chuckle as Makellos sat upon the throne in the newly repaired throne room of the palace.

Makellos smiled at the seven little men assembled before him. "It is thanks to all of you," he said. "I am here because of you, and I would not trade my time with you for anything in the world."

The little men smiled back, but Makellos could see the sadness in their eyes. He was in the palace once more, with servants and responsibilities and a kingdom that needed him. His own heart had ached when he thought of them returning to their distant cottage, away from him, away from the love and the life they had built together. Which was why he had assembled them all before him now.

"I have something to ask of you," he said. "I have learned so much from each of you, with so much more still to glean. I cannot possibly rule this kingdom all by myself, nor do I wish to, for it is important that the people have a voice. You each have your own areas of expertise, and I believe your knowledge and compassion would be invaluable to Falchovari. As such, I would like to ask if all seven of you would stay here with me, as my royal advisors?"

A dropped pin could have been heard in the stunned silence that fell over the throne room. Makellos felt his breath catch as seven pairs of eyes stared back at him. Had he said something wrong? Would they decide to leave him and return to the simple home they had known for so long? Did they perhaps no longer want to be with him now that he had taken the crown?

Then Dagobert gave a great whoop. "Yes!" he shouted, and sprinted over to Makellos to throw his arms around him tightly.

The silence broken, the others surged forward as well, with cheers of delight. Makellos slid off of his throne and onto his knees so he could embrace all of them as they crowded around him. "Yes, of course I will, Snow, I mean, your highness! I mean, your majesty!" Der said, stumbling all over himself.

"It would be an honor to serve you," Hardwic said, sweeping into a grand bow.

Tears of joy filled Makellos' eyes as their warmth and love surrounded him, pulling them close, kissing each of them in turn. "Thank you. Thank you so much. I love you, all of you, with all of my heart."

"We love you too, Snow," said Sigurd.

"Never had my cock sucked by a king before," Sigmund added, and Der and Hardwic shot him a reproachful glare.

"You really think we have what it takes to run a kingdom?" Grim asked, a smirk curving up the corner of his lips. "You sure you ain't doin' this just to keep us all around in your bed?"

"Why can't it be both?" Makellos said, giving him a wink and a bright smile back. "After all, it's only fair."

Epilogue

Thus ended the reign of the evil Queen, and a new era of prosperity began under the good King Makellos and his seven royal advisors. Almost immediately, King Makellos had the palace storehouses inventoried, and the excess food was sent to all corners of the kingdom to help those who had been suffering most under the famine. Fresh fruit and vegetables, ground flour, salted meats, cheeses, and even spices were sent far and wide. It would take time for the country to regain the prosperity it had once had, but Makellos knew it would be easier for everyone to do the work with a full belly and no worry about where the next meal would come from.

Much had changed in the twenty-two years that the little men were away from the city. Grimwald and Der's families were gone, as was the acting troupe Bernhardt had once traveled with. Makellos knew that their losses were sometimes heavy upon their hearts, but they still lived and loved every day and did their best to improve the lives of all of the citizens of Falchovari.

Sigurd and Sigmund's family had returned to Hallin shortly after the brothers were taken. Letters were sent to them informing them that the two were alive and well, and plans were made for them to come to Falchovari soon for a visit.

Sigmund sought out Florian, the fiancé he had been forced to leave behind twenty-two years ago. Florian was married now, with four beautiful children, and Sigmund became their dear uncle.

Dagobert worked with scholars and local storytellers at the behest of the king, and, over the course of several years, he wrote the history of Falchovari, the reign of the evil Queen Schön, and the rise of King Makellos to the throne. There was a search for his family as well, to find if they were still in the country. That information was never found, but Dagobert knew he always had a family in the six little men and the king who loved him so dearly.

It was while searching the archives that he happened upon a family tree that he brought to Makellos' attention. One of the merchant nobility families had a son, the name written in flowing script, with a wife and daughter attached to it. *Hardwic.*

"You had a noble title this whole time? Why did you not tell me?" Makellos asked Hardwic, and the little round man flushed.

"Forgive me, your majesty. It was always my desire to serve at court, despite what I knew of the Queen. I thought that my family's station would be enough to protect me from her scrutiny. However, I was obviously very wrong." Hardwic's usual bright demeanor was serious and somber. "I was ashamed of my views and the things I did to try to win favor, and the loss of my wife and daughter were bitter pills to swallow. The mines, well... They were a chance for me to start over again, to re-evaluate what I wanted and who I was. Perhaps it was wicked of me to keep it a secret from everyone, but I wanted to take the second chance I had been given."

"But you told Der?" Makellos asked kindly.

"Yes. He recognized me right away, but he didn't say anything all of those years we lived together."

"And he still loves you," Makellos said. "As do I."

Hardwic gave him a beaming smile. "Then I am the happiest of men."

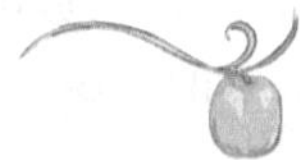

Under the new king, Falchovari began to flourish once more. The seven little men took on their roles as Makellos' advisors with aplomb. There were many changes to be made to help the country thrive again. They worked on plans to reinvigorate the kingdom's various trades, from lumber to mining to medicine, as well as to establish more education options for the children of both the rich and the poor.

Makellos worked closely with Ulrich, Zel, and the Thieves Guild to use magical enchantments on the fruits and vegetables of the kingdom to help them grow larger and faster. The kingdoms of Falchovari and Hallin forged many strong treaties and trades under the reigns of King Makellos and King Adalwin, who became friends and were both well-respected leaders.

And throughout the lands, love continued to grow in its many forms. Deep in the forest, an archer and his wolf created their own family. In a tower outside the city, a sorcerer and his beloved made magic flourish. Two step-brothers became lovers and avengers against brutality. Two elves and their quiet shoemaker basked in their hard-earned peace. A prince and a vigilante together built a new life of love and justice. A cursed royal heir found love and became a king. A shadow geist found freedom, his name, and his Heart. And the fairest of all shared all of himself with his seven true loves. Each story was unique, but the love created between them was everlasting. And they all lived happily ever after.

Thank you for reading *Snow White and the Seven Little Miners*! Each book set in the GriMM fairytale world can be read as a standalone and contains its own Happily Ever After story. But we do recommend reading each one, as the tales are connected to each other in multiple magical ways.

Little Red Riding Hood by TJ Rose
Zel by Amanda Meuwissen
Hansel and Gerhardt by W.H. Lockwood
The Elves and the Shoemaker by Emory Winters
Cinder by D.N. Bryn
The Frog Prince by A.M. Rose
Rumpelstilzchen by Sam Northman
Snow White and the Seven Little Miners by Kit Barrie

If you enjoyed this book, please consider leaving a review. Reviews from readers like you are the life's blood of the independent author.

About the Author

Kit Barrie (she/her) was raised by pirates in a traveling carnival where she learned how to fly and to weave fantasy into reality. She identifies as chaotic bisexual, with good intentions and questionable methods. She lives in an utterly unfantastical state in the Midwestern United States with some food goblins who might just be cats gobblin' food.

Please visit www.kitbarrie.com or scan the QR code below for more information on Kit and her other available titles.

ADDITIONAL TITLES BY KIT BARRIE

<u>The Queerly Classic Collection</u>
The Prince on the Lake: A Queer YA Fairy Tale
Midnight Companion: An MM Retelling of The Legend of Sleepy
Hollow
X Marks the Spot: A Gay Retelling of Treasure Island

<u>The Hanenea'a Chronicles</u>
The Goblin Twins
A Study in Scholar
The Gift

<u>Standalones</u>
Where the Sky Meets the Sea: An MM Mer Steampunk Romance
Spinning Out of Control: An MM Monster Romance (Monster
Match series)
Swimming in Grief: An MM Monster Romance (Monster Match
Season 2 series)
Across Space and Time (Tales From the Tarot series)

Please consider leaving a review on Amazon, Goodreads, or other
book review site. Reviews are extremely important for independent
authors and are always appreciated.